The zipper on Peri's raincoat was stuck. Wouldn't you know! Trapped in a soggy old raincoat, just when she needed to feel her best.

"Troubles?"

Peri looked up into a pair of clear silver-gray eyes that were startlingly light against the man's sun-darkened skin.

"Makes one yearn for the dark ages, doesn't it?" he said in a pleasantly deep masculine voice. "No zippers back then. I doubt they even bothered with buttons. Hold your coat firmly and I'll work it back on it's track."

Peri realized that he wasn't waiting for permission. Alarmed, she grabbed the coat and held it away from the soft fullness of her bosom.

"Please forget it!" she said. "I'm late for an appointment."

"Steady," he soothed, his wink mischievous. "You'll see . . . I have the hands of a magician."

Dear Reader,

Although our culture is always changing, the desire to love and be loved is a constant in every woman's heart. Silhouette Romances reflect that desire, sweeping you away with books that will make you laugh and cry, poignant stories that will move you time and time again.

This year we're featuring Romances with a playful twist. Remember those fun-loving heroines who always manage to get themselves into tricky predicaments? You'll enjoy reading about their escapades in Silhouette Romances by Brittany Young, Debbie Macomber, Annette Broadrick and Rita Rainville.

We're also publishing Romances by many of your all-time favorites such as Ginna Gray, Dixie Browning, Laurie Paige and Joan Hohl. Your overwhelming reaction to these authors has served as a touchstone for us, and we're pleased to bring you more books with Silhouette's distinctive medley of charm, wit and—above all—*romance*. I hope you enjoy this book, and the many stories to come.

Sincerely,

Rosalind Noonan
Senior Editor
SILHOUETTE BOOKS

BEVERLY TERRY
Before the Loving

Silhouette *Romance*

Published by Silhouette Books New York

America's Publisher of Contemporary Romance

For my mother—
my most faithful reader

SILHOUETTE BOOKS
300 E. 42nd St., New York, N.Y. 10017

Copyright © 1986 by Beverly Haaf

ISBN: 0-373-08414-5

First Silhouette Books printing February 1986

America's Publisher of Contemporary Romance

Printed in the U.S.A.

BEVERLY TERRY

lives in New Jersey. She and her husband met while attending college, and she taught elementary school before staying home to raise a family. Although she has written magazine features and newspaper articles on a variety of subjects, her main love has always been fiction writing— mysteries, the occult and, of course, romance. She also enjoys doing portrait painting, but she says that she is fictional in her painting, too, as the portraits rarely turn out to look like the real person.

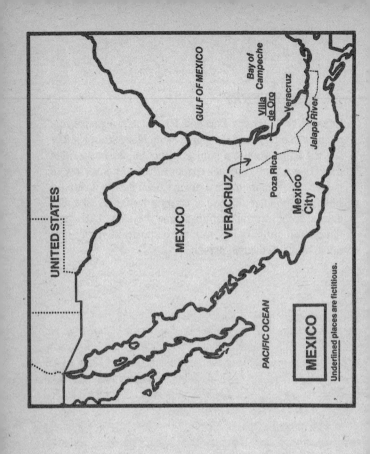

MEXICO

Underlined places are fictitious.

Chapter One

"Hi, Peri," greeted Janet Maxwell, a plump brunette who also worked in credit at Raymond's department store. As they entered the bustling office, Janet, wet from the early morning shower, asked fretfully, "How come you were prepared with a raincoat when this was supposed to be a sunny June day? Are you really so efficient, or do you have a crystal ball?"

Glad to think of something besides her impending meeting with her department head, Perdita Brendan laughed, light dancing in her smoky, violet-blue eyes. "Tea leaves. I read them at breakfast instead of the newspaper."

"I believe it," Janet said, laughing. "Say..." Voice dropping to a conspiratorial hush, she motioned across the room. "Take a look at our visitor. Is he a hunk of a man, or is he not!"

Peri looked, seeing a tall stranger talking with the store's senior accountant. Carrying his broad-shouldered,

athletic frame with the ease of one born to authority, he
was about thirty-five, his dark brown, wavy hair combed
back from a deeply tanned, hawk-nosed face. Something the accountant said amused him and he threw back
his head and laughed, the gesture bold and free and totally masculine. Peri suddenly envisioned him as a buc-
caneer—afraid of nothing, daring everything, caring only
for the zest of the game.

As Janet moved on to the ladies' room, Peri realized
she had been staring at the man as if mesmerized. Annoyed, she reminded herself that she should be getting
ready for her meeting. Stepping to the coat tree, she gave
her raincoat zipper a pull. It slid midway to her chest,
then jammed. She struggled, then realized it was truly
stuck.

"Oh, no!" she wailed softly. With the zipper caught as
it was, she could neither pull the garment off over her
head, nor work it down over her hips. Wouldn't you
know! Trapped in a soggy old raincoat, just when she
needed to feel at her best.

"Troubles?" inquired a pleasantly deep, masculine
voice.

Peri looked up into the face of the stranger. Close up,
he still possessed stunning good looks, only now she
could see imperfections that added strangely to his appeal. A slight bump, as if his nose had once been broken, marred the bold, aristocratic lines of his features,
and a scar hooking into one eyebrow gave it a quizzical
tilt. His eyes were a clear, silver gray, startlingly light
against his sun-darkened skin.

He assessed her predicament. "I see . . . stuck zipper."
His grin crinkled the corners of his eyes and cut a pleas-
ing crevice in one lean cheek. "Makes one yearn for the
dark ages, doesn't it? No zippers back then. I doubt they

even bothered much with buttons—just good honest laces. Hold your coat firmly, and I'll work it back on its track."

Peri realized he wasn't waiting for permission. Alarmed, she hastily held the coat away from the soft fullness of her bosom as he gripped the zipper toggle.

Of necessity, he stood extremely close and she could smell the clean, woodsy spice of his after-shave. She glanced down at his hands. They were lean and powerful, the dark hair at his wrists appearing primitive against the urbane whiteness of his shirt cuffs. She felt the teasing tug against the fabric of her coat and suddenly felt as if he were about to strip her naked.

Face flaming at her imagination, she wondered why she had allowed his interference. "Please, forget it," she told him. "I'm late for an appointment."

"Steady," he soothed, his wink mischievous. "You'll see... I have the fingers of a magician."

"Please, no." Intending to push him away, her palms closed about the warmth of his hands, inadvertently charging the moment with increased intimacy. She recoiled as if burned.

"There!" Miraculously, the zipper was free.

"Thank you." She was aware that her palms still tingled from contact with him.

"My pleasure." Before she could stop him, he was presumptuously slipping her out of her coat, making no attempt to mask his interest as her figure was revealed, the trim lines of her turquoise linen dress discreetly displaying her slender waist and the lush roundness of her breasts.

"Well, now! You're certainly all set to go knock 'em dead. Is it a job you're after?" He gave her a devastatingly brilliant smile.

Peri froze. All too often she had seen that same kind of star-dazzling smile on the face of her father, the stage actor, Leslie Brendan. She had worshiped him until she was thirteen, when the shocking facts surrounding his death in an auto accident proved he had been nothing but a glib, shallow womanizer. Although this stranger looked nothing like her red-headed father, his smile seemed to advertise the same careless charm.

Unaware of the chill that had come over her, he leaned against her desk, arms folded, as if preparing for an extended stay. Even in that indolent position, he towered over her. His eyebrow with the fishhook scar lifted. "Is it a job you're after?" he repeated, his tone pleasant, yet managing to suggest he was accustomed to getting his answer the first time around.

"I already have a job," she snapped, not explaining that her meeting would probably determine whether or not she would keep it. "Now, if you don't mind—" His legs, heavily muscled thighs taut against the lightweight fabric of his trousers, were angled so she would have to almost climb over them to hang up her coat.

Not moving, he started to say something else, his tone jocular, then his words trailed off. He peered deeply into Peri's eyes as if really seeing her for the first time. An expression she couldn't read flashed over his features. She decided her dislike of him must have registered.

His manner became stiff. "Good luck," he said shortly, and strode off.

Peri stared after him, startled by the change in his manner, yet relieved he was gone. His presence had been oddly disturbing, and on that morning especially, she needed a clear head. Checking the clock, she belatedly realized she had no time left to comb her hair or check her makeup.

Mr. Sauer, a prim, bifocaled man nearing retirement, waited for her in the doorway of his office. "Miss Brendan," he said with malicious glee, "I have informed Mrs. Raymond of your behavior yesterday. Instead of you keeping your appointment with me, she wants you in her office at once."

Hiding her dismay, Peri kept her head held high as she wove through the desks of her fellow employees. Although her face was composed, her knees trembled as she mounted the stairs to the glass-walled executive mezzanine.

Having worked in the store just eight months, Peri considered Estelle Raymond more of a legend than an actual person. President of several domestic and foreign corporations, the woman visited the store that bore her family name on an irregular basis. To date, Peri had only seen her from a distance, but she had often looked up at the glass wall and wondered if Estelle was there, peering down like a queen bee surveying her workers. Reaching the fabled door, Peri drew a deep breath. Of all times, she thought while knocking, why did Estelle have to be around when she had landed herself into trouble?

Following the command to enter, Peri found herself facing a slender figure enthroned behind a heavily carved desk.

"Sit down, please, Miss Brendan," directed the vibrant woman whose chin-length gray hair was the only concession to her nearly sixty years. She reminded Peri of Lauren Bacall. With a sidelong smile and catlike, slanted eyes, Estelle Raymond had the air of confidence that comes from being unafraid of making mistakes and never making the same mistake twice. She was, Peri decided with shrewd insight, the kind of woman who would be a loyal friend, but a fearful enemy.

After Peri took a seat, Estelle studied her for a long, silent moment, then jumped immediately to the main point. "Miss Brendan, is it true that yesterday you told your department manager, Ward Sauer, that he should be fired?"

Peri flushed. "Not exactly, Mrs. Raymond."

"Suppose you explain."

Grateful she was at least being given a chance to tell her side of the story, Peri forced her voice to reflect calm despite the wild thumping of her heart.

"I presented Mr. Sauer with a report outlining the innovations I had instituted in the credit department. After reading it, he agreed I deserved a raise, but said that money was short. If I was to receive a pay increase, one of my department co-workers would have to be let go. I was supposed to decide which worker that should be." Remembered anger darkened Peri's eyes to the indigo of a sky before a storm. "His proposal was nothing but a shabby trick, Mrs. Raymond. He thought I would be naive enough to immediately say I didn't want a raise badly enough to cause a friend to lose her job."

"And were you that naive?" asked Estelle, clearly intrigued.

"Certainly not!" Peri sat taller. "I told him that his proposal must be a test, because he surely wouldn't fire anyone on my say-so. He insisted he was serious. The way he was trying to manipulate me was infuriating!" Peri unconsciously clenched her hands. "I lost my temper, but didn't let it show. I asked if the person to be fired should be one who failed to live up to the responsibilities of his position. He said he guessed so. That's when I said what I shouldn't have. I told him that the determination of who should be fired belonged exclusively to management, and since he was so eager to hand over the decision to me, a mere clerk, the person in the department not living up to job responsibilities was *him*."

Estelle's eyes widened, then she threw back her head and laughed. "How like myself at your age, Miss Brendan!" Then she sobered. "Even if Mr. Sauer wasn't playing fair, your response was insolent. Have you considered that I may have called you up to personally terminate your employment?"

Peri swallowed, but met the woman's gaze squarely. "I have."

"What would you do then?"

"I'd get another job. A better one."

Estelle laughed again, her expression approving. "Miss Brendan, I have no intention of letting you go. You can be valuable to me." She lifted a manila folder that Peri recognized as the report she had presented to Mr. Sauer. "I've read this and was impressed by your initiative. I was equally impressed by your work in editing and arranging photographs for this store's twenty-fifth anniversary booklet. I'm convinced you're the person to solve a problem that has put me at my wit's end."

Dumbfounded, Peri learned that Mrs. Raymond wanted her to act as secretary to her twenty-year-old granddaughter, Karen. In addition to the job paying far more than what she had hoped to gain from a raise, it also meant traveling to a magnificent villa owned by Mrs. Raymond in Veracruz, Mexico.

Estelle explained, "Despite her youth, Karen, who is a talented photographer, has won a commission to do a book about Indian artifacts unearthed in Veracruz. Because of my villa's location, Karen has been staying with family members while she works. The situation should be ideal, yet in a year's time, the girl had made little progress."

The woman's strong, dogmatic voice faltered as she continued to speak of her granddaughter. "I have learned that the hundreds of photographs she has taken for the project are in chaos in her workroom. The failure of the book to progress is only one example of the disorganization that rules her life. Karen is a sweet, sensitive young woman, but she allows herself to suffer moods of depression that concern me deeply. I believe you can help her."

Peri felt she was being thrust into a situation she couldn't handle. "Mrs. Raymond, I don't think I'm the kind of person you're seeking."

"I disagree. Your work has proven your rare ability to analyze situations, solve problems and see tasks through to conclusion—the very skills Karen lacks. All I will expect from you is your assistance in getting her photographs ready for book publication. I'm convinced that when she sees herself master this aspect of her life, it will aid in other areas as well." Estelle spoke with such conviction that Peri's arguments died on her tongue. "Also, Miss Brendan, your background has probably made you sympathetic to the artistic temperament. Where most take-charge persons would lose patience with Karen, I believe you will be more understanding."

A frown drew Peri's golden brows together. "You mean because my father was in the theater?" Leslie Brendan had been an award-winning actor, but Peri, preferring to forget the painful past, had told no one in the office of the connection. "How did you know?"

Estelle cocked her head. "It's not the result of prying, if that's what you think." She pointed to a framed landscape of an ocher-colored Moorish-style house set along an exotic, palm-lined beach. "That is Villa de Oro, where you will stay with Karen. I'm having a section rebuilt by an American construction firm. The man in charge of the work crew, Harris Logan, told me that an old friend of his, Perdita Brendan, daughter of the famed Leslie Brendan, worked in my store. When Ward Sauer brought your name to my attention, I remembered what Harris said."

Peri mulled over the name, *Harris Logan*, then brightened. "Oh, yes! When Harris and I were about twelve years old, his father was head of the stage crew where my father was playing. It was summer and we hung around the theater together. I haven't seen him since."

"Then your stay at the villa will be a reunion, because Harris is still working there." Manner becoming crisp, Estelle took up her pen and began outlining travel arrangements and other details, the force of her personality sweeping Peri along so swiftly that it wasn't until she had already been scheduled to fly to Veracruz that following Monday that she realized she had never formally accepted the job. Somehow, Estelle Raymond allowed little choice except to follow along. No wonder she had carved herself so secure a place in business.

On her way to the door, Peri passed by the windows overlooking the office. She saw her desk, her raincoat still lying where the stranger had placed it. For an instant she remembered their disturbing encounter, then the thought was gone and she was concentrating on nothing except the job that lay ahead.

Watching Peri leave, Estelle Raymond sighed deeply, looking every year of her age. How risky was it to play God? Perhaps she would someday bitterly regret the decision she had made that morning, but it was too late to worry. Her plan was in motion.

A week later found Peri seated in a station wagon being swiftly driven away from the airport in the Mexican state of Veracruz. She stared at her driver, finding it difficult to believe that the radiant young woman could be Karen Raymond. Canary-bright in a yellow sundress, Karen had a neat, energetic figure and the rounded, pretty face of a Hummel figurine. She looked as if she had never suffered a depressed day in her life.

Turning merry brown eyes toward Peri, Karen giggled. "We had a fight over you up at the villa. Harris wanted to meet your plane, but since you're my secretary, I figured I was the one who should play taxi. Besides, you and Harris already know one another, so I should have my chance to get to know you, right?"

"Right," laughed Peri, a bit confused by the rush of Karen's words. "At least, I knew Harris once. Now we could probably pass in a crowd and not recognize one another." She was remembering a thin, pug-nosed boy with a nervous squint.

"He'd know you all right," returned Karen, flashing Peri a look. "All week he's talked of nothing except his memories of the beautiful Peri Brendan with the red-gold hair and purple eyes."

"Purple?"

"Okay, so maybe he said violet, but I like to be dramatic. Of course, I was thinking that the pretty swan Harris once knew could have grown into an ugly duckling. Estelle said you were a knockout, but she's famous for distorting facts." Karen took her eyes off the road again, not slackening speed as she scrutinized Peri with an impish grin. "She was right. You're everything she claimed."

Peri felt relief when they entered the city of Veracruz and Karen slowed the car, maneuvering through a congestion of pushcart vendors, bike riders and pedestrians, many of them dressed in native Mexican garb. As they traveled along Shoreline Boulevard, Karen stretched a dimpled arm toward the gulf, which lay mirror-flat in the calm evening. "Over there is the marina where Marc keeps his boat," she said, not bothering to explain who Marc was.

Although it was nearly eight o'clock, the light from the lowering sun remained strong, enabling Peri to see the sights—the modern lighthouse, the colorful bazaar and the landmark of an old fort that formed a low, impressive skyline far out in the water.

Deciding that Karen's driving must be more skillful than it appeared, Peri relaxed as they left the city behind. "Besides Harris and you, who else lives at the villa?"

"There's Aunt Josepha—Estelle's sister, so she's really a great aunt, and Uncle Theo. There's also a chance Marc might show up for dinner." She glanced at Peri. "I guess you know we have dinner late in this part of the world. The siesta gives everyone a midday rest, so late evenings are the rule. What's the frown for? You hungry now?"

"I'm wondering who Marc is. You've mentioned him twice."

"Oh, he's just my devastatingly handsome older brother, that's who," responded Karen, a lilt in her voice. "Gee, you're still frowning! You don't like good-looking guys?"

"Oh, no objection at all!" Peri felt a thrill at the thought of meeting an attractive man. She supposed most women her age had been in and out of love a dozen times, yet none of her admirers had struck that vital spark. So far, she was holding out for true romance.

She returned to Karen's question. "I'm just surprised to learn you have a brother. From what your grandmother said, I assumed you were her only grandchild."

"Estelle probably didn't mention Marc because he wasn't supposed to be here. But yesterday, instead of going to Paris to report on one of her factories, he got smart and decided to take a vacation. Being her right-hand man doesn't mean he always has to jump to her tune."

Sensing friction, Peri ventured, "Sounds as if things aren't necessarily smooth between you and your grandmother."

Karen's voice hardened. "She wants to run everyone's life. She even tried to pick out a husband for me! When I found a fellow of my own, she naturally thought he wasn't good enough. She's going to dance with joy when she learns I've just broken the engagement."

Peri remembered her own strong impression of Estelle's imposing manner, but all she said was, "I can't imagine her being pleased if you're unhappy. She cares deeply for you and only has your—"

"Best interest in mind," mocked Karen, anticipating the rest of the sentence. The eyes she turned to Peri suddenly glittered with resentment. "You're the latest of her little schemes. Helping me finish that photography book is suppose to wave a magic wand and solve all my other problems as well."

It was becoming clear that Karen wasn't the carefree person she had first appeared. She seemed so touchingly vulnerable that Peri, although only two years older, felt maternal.

"You may be right about your grandmother's attitude, Karen," she said sympathetically, "But that still leaves you with a book to finish. Since I'm here, you might as well make use of me." Her tone was encouraging. "Tomorrow morning, first thing, let's start getting your photos in order."

Karen thought for a moment. "I suppose you're right. Yes, of course you are." Expression transformed, she smiled. "Peri Brendan, I think I'm going to like you." She pointed ahead. "Look—your first view of the villa."

Peri gasped with delight. The villa, with its red-tiled roof, iron-laced balconies and ornately cut windows, was situated on a rise facing the gulf, its yellow walls gilded by the declining sun. Karen guided the station wagon up a palm-shaded drive and came to a stop under a porte cochere. The iron-studded front door was opened by a stout, smiling Indian woman. An Indian boy wearing shorts and a yellow T-shirt, with a picture of a bunch of bananas and the English message, Best Of The Bunch, scampered down the steps to the car, where he started to unload the luggage.

Karen introduced Peri to the boy, Luis, and to his aunt, Concepcion, the villa's cook and housekeeper, then led the way inside and up a wide staircase to a hallway where open arches overlooked gardens on the floor below. Flinging open a door, Karen showed Peri her bedroom, which had green damask walls, an ornately carved bed and a window with a breathtaking view of the gulf.

While Peri was admiring the view, Luis, puffing and panting, arrived with her luggage. "Luis!" Karen chided affectionately, ruffling his coarse, jet-black hair. "You shouldn't try carrying everything at once. You'll stretch your arms out of their sockets."

"I am eleven, and I am strong," he boasted with only a trace of accent. His grin showed strong, square teeth. As he left the room, Karen returned her attention to Peri. "Well, how do you like it?"

"Like it? Karen, I love it!"

Pleased, Karen outlined the evening ahead, saying there would be an hour to bathe and prepare for dinner. "When you come down, I'll introduce you to my aunt and uncle. And if he's coming, Marc should have arrived, although he's so unpredictable, who can be sure?"

"I thought he was your grandmother's right-hand man. I wouldn't have expected her to tolerate unpredictable behavior."

"In business Marc can be counted on, he's only capricious in other areas." Karen gave Peri a sidelong look. "I suppose I should warn you about my brother. Beautiful woman always see him as a challenge." Her expression became playful. "I've got to tell you, he has no intention of getting caught."

"What makes him so special?" Peri was intrigued even though she mistrusted Karen's obvious idolization of her brother.

"Well, first, he's handsome." Karen ticked off points on her fingers. "Second, he has an adorable manner...charisma, I suppose. Third, he's rich. Oh, yes— fourth, there is the romance of his great tragedy."

"Tragedy?"

Karen gave an airy wave. "Yes, the tragedy of a heart so badly broken that he'll never risk having it happen again!"

Peri got a fleeting impression that Karen might be deliberately glossing over something significant, but the girl was racing on.

"The thing is, for years he's been the most incurable playboy imaginable, wooing a different female at every turn. I suppose you think you'll be the exception, and it will suit him fine to have you try to prove it. He loves that game, but I warn you, it's hopeless."

Unawares, Karen had described exactly the kind of man Peri detested, but the girl was so proudly confident of her brother's fatal charm that Peri hid her disappointment and merely rolled her eyes. "Thanks for the warning."

Karen laughed. "Oh, Peri Brendan! I admit I wanted to dislike you simply because Estelle picked you out, but now, I'm awfully glad you're here!" With a wink, the girl was gone.

Thoughts busy, Peri laid out her clothes for dinner, efficiently unpacking and putting away her other clothing at the same time. She noticed that her sweater had a loose button. As she took a needle and thread from her sewing kit, she recalled the voice of the handsome stranger speaking of buttons, zippers and laces. Disconcerted, she pricked her finger.

"Damn!" she whispered under her breath. This wasn't the first time he had intruded upon her thoughts and it exasperated her. If the headlong rush of planning for the trip hadn't kept her away from the office, she supposed she might have weakened and made an attempt to learn who he was. But, for what purpose? Although there had been something compelling about him, she was convinced he wasn't her kind of man. Pricked finger to her lips, she resolutely turned her thoughts to Karen.

In the brief time she had known the girl, her mercurial temperament had already caught her off guard several times. Although Peri liked her enormously, she'd be kidding herself to imagine Karen easy to deal with. Estelle had estimated it would take a month to finish the book. Looking ahead, Peri couldn't help wondering what her relationship with Karen would be like by then.

An hour later, wearing an orchid-colored skirt and blouse and high-heeled sandals, Peri descended the

staircase. A leisurely bath had refreshed her and she was
pleased with her appearance—except for her hair, which
the tropical humidity had turned into a springy mass of
blush-gold, gypsy curls. Abandoning attempts at sleek
sophistication, she had put aside her pearls and fastened
golden hoops in her ears and clasped a matching brace-
let about a slender wrist. Now, reaching the entry court,
she found Karen waiting in the company of a stocky,
blond-bearded man.

Even though Peri had prepared herself for disappointment, her mouth dropped at the sight of Marc, who
was supposed to be so fabulous. True, he was nice looking, with a fresh wholesome appearance, his complexion
sunburned, his hazel eyes watching her approach with
flattering attention. But it was next to impossible to believe this bearded teddy bear of a fellow could ever impress anyone as a suave Casanova.

Karen was dressed in pale blue, her thick, dark hair,
which had been braided that afternoon, now rippling
down her back *Alice in Wonderland* fashion. Brother and
sister bore no family resemblance, yet as they stood side
by side like dolls atop a wedding cake, they seemed to
belong together.

"Peri, don't you know me?" asked the man, stepping
forward. "It's me—Harris."

"Goodness!" Feeling utterly foolish, Peri threw a
hand to her face, her thoughts of the last few moments
tumbling in confusion. "Of course—Harris!" Delighted, she hurried to him, hands extended to grip his.
"The last time I saw you, you were a skinny, freckled
twelve-year-old. How could I know you with a beard?"

His laughter joined hers. Eyes taking in the way the
orchid skirt and blouse clung to her curves, he blurted,
"If the years have brought changes in me, why—look at

you!'' He blushed furiously, and Peri remembered how bashful he had been as a youngster.

They talked of old times, then Harris said, ''Karen tells me you're doing office work. When I heard you were at Raymond's, I assumed you were modeling in their fashion shows, using it as a springboard to follow your father's footsteps into acting.''

''Not me,'' Peri answered quickly, remembering how the shameful disclosure of Leslie Brendan's string of mistresses had nearly destroyed her mother. ''Theater life holds no appeal for me.''

At that moment Karen's Aunt Josepha and Uncle Theo appeared and were introduced.

''Might as well go in to dinner before Concepcion blows a gasket about the fish getting cold,'' boomed Josepha cheerfully. Although she had the same gray hair and slanted eyes of her sister, in every other respect she was the opposite of the refined Estelle—her dress a glaring red, her manner brash and unpolished.

''Marc might show up,'' cautioned Theo, a bald, mild little man.

''The quickest way to make him appear is to start without him,'' reasoned Josepha, smiling broadly at Peri. ''I bet this little gal is starved after one of those skimpy airline snacks. Let's go eat.''

The matter settled, the group entered the dining room where leaded glass windows overlooked a garden of roses. Soup and salad were followed by a main course of fish in a delicious herb-butter sauce. Wine was available and Peri noticed that Harris filled his glass repeatedly. Josepha dominated the conversation, speaking of a trip she and Theo had planned for later that month. Peri learned they were anthropologists who studied ancient Indian cultures.

Dessert and coffee were served in the lounge, and by that time Peri could feel a strange tension between Karen and Harris. It was almost as if each tried to pretend the other one wasn't present. When the gregarious Josepha left the room for a moment, she left behind a pained, stilted silence. Speaking to fill the gap, Peri said to Theo, "The villa has such lovely gardens! How many are there?"

He beamed. "Eight altogether. Three in interior courtyards and five outside." Previously, when Josepha allowed him to get a word in sideways, he had mentioned an interest in horticulture. "And that, of course, doesn't include those without formal boundaries."

"The terrace garden just outside the lounge is especially pretty at night," interjected Karen. Turning to Harris, she suggested with artificial brightness, "Why don't you take Peri out to see it?"

Harris appeared startled: Peri realized it was the first time Karen had addressed him directly since before dinner. After a hesitation, he asked, "Well, Peri—want to?"

Glad to escape the air of tension, she nodded. "Yes, I would."

As they got up to leave, Theo switched on the television, the soft, liquid rhythm of the announcer's Spanish fading as they stepped through the French doors and out into a night filled with the whisper of palms stirring in the breeze and the soft, distant sound of waves caressing the beach. Peri lifted her head to a velvet-blue sky sequined with stars.

"It's so beautiful," she murmured. "I'm only scheduled to be here a short while, and already, I regret the idea of leaving." Lowering her gaze, she looked at Harris. The light from the lounge revealed an unhappy expression on his bearded face.

"Harris, what's going on—what's wrong?"

He sighed. "What you said about hating to leave—that's how I felt myself until a few days ago. Then, everything changed." Abruptly, he shook himself like a wet dog. "Hey, my maudlin ramblings aren't making sense are they?" he apologized, squinting. "Guess I overdid the wine at dinner."

Suddenly Peri clearly saw the youth she had once known. His gawky form had filled out, but he was still puppy shy and very sweet. She didn't know how the beard could have fooled her for even a second. This was her old friend from that long-ago summer.

He took her hand. "Peri, remember that summer?"

"I was just thinking about it."

It was too dark to be certain, but Peri felt sure he was blushing again as he said, "Did you know you were the first girl I ever kissed? I suppose you realize I had an awful crush on you."

Peri had only a dim recall of that childish kiss, but knew it would be unkind to admit it. "Maybe I had a bit of a crush on you, too," she told him, shading the truth.

He chuckled. "How simple life seemed then! But what I'm driving at is that I always thought of you as a special pal. When I heard you were coming here to the villa, I decided to ask—"

What Harris was about to say was forgotten as sounds, like the thrashing of a large animal, came from the far side of the garden. Too startled to be alarmed, Peri stared blankly as the figure of a man burst from the shadows.

Barefoot, dressed in a T-shirt and jeans rolled to his knees, he bounded with agile swiftness up the steps leading to the terrace. As he moved into the light coming from the lounge, Peri gasped, recognizing him as the stranger she had met the week before.

"Marc!" exclaimed Karen happily, throwing open the French doors. "Where in the world did you come from?"

"Waded up from the beach," he explained in that deep voice Peri remembered so well. Then, she was stunned to hear him add, "I never should have sailed in, because it got me here too late to welcome my darling Peri." He stretched out his hand, and even in the dimness, his smile was dazzling. "Sweetheart—did I frighten you? Of course I did. I'm sorry."

Before Peri could even try to make sense out of what Marc was saying, he had crossed the distance between them, his form large and imposing as he enfolded her in his arms. Swinging her around as if she were weightless, he put his broad, well-muscled back to Karen and Harris.

Peri stared up into his shadowy face in helpless astonishment. Although his greeting had been warmly affectionate, the words he spoke next were gritted through clenched teeth. In a voice so low only she could hear, he glared down at her, muttering, "You follow my lead, you little hired troublemaker, or I'll break every bone in your body."

To demonstrate the force behind his threat, he tightened his arms, the merciless steel bands crushing the breath from her lungs. Through the agonizing pressure she heard him exclaim for the benefit of his audience, "My darling Peri, how wonderful to hold you close again!"

His grip loosened a fraction so she could breathe, then he took her breath once more as his handsome face descended, his lips claiming hers.

Chapter Two

Dizzied from the shock of his forceful embrace, Peri half stumbled as Marc turned her so they faced the others. He stood behind her, one arm firmly about her waist, pressing her slim body back against his. His other hand had captured her wrist. She realized that although the pose probably appeared natural and affectionate, he was permitting her no more freedom than a puppet.

"Peri...how sneaky!" cried Karen, giggling deliciously. "The entire time I raved about my brother, you never even hinted you knew him. But now, I see you do— and apparently, *quite* well!"

The warning pressure of Marc's grip on her wrist reminded Peri of his command to follow his lead. Head clearing, her inclination was to burst out in indignant fury at his unwarranted behavior and to demand an explanation, yet she hesitated. Obviously something was going on that she didn't understand. With the others present she couldn't believe she was in real danger, so for the time being it seemed more prudent to play along.

Marc's tone held indulgent amusement. "Peri never realized there was any connection between me and her employer, Estelle Raymond, did you, darling? I never explained." He had inclined his head and she felt his breath warm against her cheek, stirring the tendrils that curled in front of her ear. "Also, I took her to places where it was unlikely to run into people who might disclose my identity."

"But why keep it secret?" puzzled Karen.

Marc's shrug communicated the movements of his body to Peri. "It seemed best if Grandmother didn't learn I was seeing an employee socially. You know how she is. She might have focused attention on Peri that would have made it difficult for her to work."

"You mean her co-workers might have suspected favoritism?" questioned Harris.

"Perhaps." Angling himself, Marc smiled down upon Peri, the planes of his forehead and jaw sharply etched in the light from the lounge. The crevice in his cheek deepened. "You do forgive my trickery, don't you, love?" His thumb dug into her waist, a nudge that demanded her favorable reply.

"Of course," came her answer. Her voice was honey, but inside, she seethed. Although she had decided to temporarily go along with his charade, she had lost all patience with being mauled. It was time for this overbearing male to learn she was not the pliable simpleton he mistook her for. While continuing to speak, she unobtrusively moved her foot backward.

"But you did give me a horrid scare," she said, fairly certain that the uplifted high heel of her shoe was now poised over his bare foot. "Why, when you leaped from the bushes, I thought I'd have heart failure. What a shock!" At the word "shock," she brought down her heel, hard.

"Hey... *what*!" Crying out, Marc released her, hopping backward, staring at her with blank disbelief. "Lord, woman—you nearly broke my foot!" Tottering to sit on a convenient bench, he winced as he lifted his foot, cradling it in both hands.

Peri wailed, "Oh, how awful of me! I'm so sorry—I get so clumsy when I'm flustered!" Her mock dismay was rewarded with a daggerlike glare from Marc.

"What's going on?" queried Theo, who had just stepped to the doorway of the lounge. "Marc, is that you? I didn't hear you arrive. What's all the yelling about?"

"Peri accidentally stepped on his foot, and it served him right," explained Karen. "He sailed from the marina and came up from the beach, jumping out at Peri and scaring her half to death. Worst of all, while they've already met before, he gave her a false name or something. She never dreamed she would meet him here."

Josepha, who had returned in time to overhear Karen's explanation, trumpeted, "What's this nonsense, Marcus? You should be ashamed. Such childish pranks from a grown man!"

"Don't scold him," interjected Peri sweetly. "I'm quite recovered, although I don't know if poor Marc is."

The veiled glance he shot at Peri was poisonous. "Poor Marc is just fine, thanks." For proof, he stood, gingerly placing his weight upon his foot.

"Thank goodness!" cried Peri as if in relief, but actually, she was thinking that while she held the upper hand, she'd better keep it. "Only, Marc, we do have to talk." She was determined to force a complete explanation from this obnoxious creature whether he wanted to give one or not. "Hiding your identity? As you can imagine, I have a basketful of questions to ask." Smiling winsomely at those clustered in the doorway, she took his hand as if to draw him off for a private conversation. "If you will excuse us?"

Exchanging amused glances, the members of the group obediently returned to the lounge. As the French doors closed, Marc fixed Peri with eyes that glinted like cold silver, growling, "You're right, Miss Brendan. We do need to talk."

Dismayed by his commanding tone, she found that despite his unimpressive costume of bare feet and surf-soaked jeans, some imperious aspect of his nature had allowed him to regain mastery over the situation. She was unable to utter even a squeak of protest as he slid an arm about her waist and conducted her from the terrace and into a clearing under the trees. Now, cut off from even the view of the others, she shivered despite the sultry air.

"Afraid to be alone with me?" came the mocking question.

"Not in the slightest," she retorted, lying. Turning to face him, she saw that the moon, which had just risen above the tops of the palms, cast an eerie glow upon his aquiline features. The angle of his scarred eyebrow lent a satanic expression to his handsome face, and the lift of his upper lip was cruel. She began to fully appreciate the size of him. Even in bare feet his height was well above average, and the breadth of his shoulders and hard-muscled chest loomed like a wall before her.

Operating on the principle that the best defense was an offense, she steadied her voice and found the courage to demand, "All right, what's the story? I cooperated with your ridiculous burlesque because I figured you must have a logical explanation. But you'd better come out with it quick, or I'm marching back to the villa to announce our prior relationship exists nowhere except in your fevered brain!''

"My, what a spitfire," he observed sarcastically, leaning back against a palm tree, folding corded arms across his chest. "So virtuous, so filled with righteous indignation. You and my grandmother make quite a pair! Karen told me a secretary had been hired for her, but it wasn't until I spoke with Grandmother yesterday that I realized something was fishy." His voice hardened. "I know the old gal pretty well, and felt something was up. I went sailing tonight to think things over, but even the sea air couldn't help me sort out my suspicions. Things didn't click into place until I came up the beach path and saw what was going on between you and Harris."

"What? There's nothing going on between Harris and me!"

He sneered. "Naturally, you plead innocent. I'm speaking, of course, of the fact that my meddling grandmother has been so dissatisfied with Karen's current choice for a husband that she's decided to take action. And you've been hired to carry out her plan."

"Wait a minute!" cried Peri, distraught. "Karen did say her grandmother had disapproved of her latest boyfriend, but what's that got to do with Harris and me?"

"Just about everything, doesn't it? Grandmother let it slip that you and Harris are old buddies. From that touching scene I witnessed on the terrace, it's obvious you two plan to take up where you left off, regardless of how Karen is hurt."

Peri blinked, feeling cast adrift in a wild and friendless sea. "You mean Harris was Karen's latest love?"

"My," he marveled nastily, "what an authentic imitation of surprise. You forget I saw how you arranged to snuggle up to him in full view of the glass where Karen sat. If you could have seen her expression as she watched the two of you—" His calm broke, fury on behalf of his sister choking his voice. Stepping away from Peri, he thrust his hands into his pockets as if afraid of what he might do with them otherwise.

Head whirling, Peri was so upset she could hardly fit her words together. "You mean that—that you think your grandmother hired me to come here and steal Harris away from your sister?"

"The answer is obvious, isn't it?" Anger back under control, his tone was rasping and chill. "I was in perfect position to see the moon-eyed adoration in his face as he gazed at you. What happened? Had you tossed the poor fellow over, and now he hopes you've come running back, never realizing my grandmother is paying for your performance?"

Peri trembled with outrage. "The last time I saw Harris, we were about twelve years old. What kind of torrid relationship do you think we were having at that age?" Then she realized she had a trump card. Haughtily, she lifted her chin. "Besides, this is all after the fact. Karen and Harris broke up before I arrived."

"What?" He looked as if he had been punched. "I don't believe it. Two weeks ago, Harris told me that he and Karen were making wedding plans."

Peri angled her head, feeling the cool weight of her earrings brush against her skin. "That may be, but several days ago, when I was nowhere around, it apparently came to an end. Do I get the blame for that, too?"

"You're lying." Dismay shook his voice. "You've got to be! Karen and Harris care for one another, I know it.

They might have had a spat, but they wouldn't have broken off for good.''

Peri shrugged, feeling meanly triumphant to see him so shaken. "Karen told me herself she had wrecked her latest romance. She didn't say who the man was, but just now on the terrace, Harris complained that things have been intolerable for the past week and he implied he wished he could leave. How else can you add it up? If he and Karen had plans for the future, things have evidently gone sour."

Marc made no reply and she looked at him sharply. His broad shoulders were slumped and he stared forlornly at the light from the lounge as if he had forgotten her presence. The anger she had felt against him softened as she realized his outrageous behavior had been prompted by the desire to protect his young sister.

"This can't be all that serious," she said gently. "If Karen and Harris really care for one another, they will reconcile their differences, but if they don't, it must be for the best. She's only twenty, with a career as a photographer ahead of her. Why the urgency to see her married?"

"You don't understand." Marc ran a hand through his dark hair, the gesture strangely weary and defeated. "Karen has a talent for photography, true, but for years, the only career she's really counted on is having a husband and a home of her own. I think it resulted from the damage she suffered when our parents died."

He turned to face Peri, his animosity forgotten as he spoke of his sister. "I was fifteen when Karen was born and our parents considered her birth a miracle. They probably lavished a lot more attention on her than most children receive. She was four years old when their deaths robbed her of that all-enveloping love. I had just started

college and could be of no help, and although our
grandmother took Karen in, there was no room in her
busy life for a little girl so hungry for affection. The situation made Karen yearn desperately for a time when she
could establish her own home and the hope of regaining
the security she had lost as a child.''

Peri was touched by the sadness of it. ''Your grandmother said Karen has bouts of depression.''

''Yes. When she was fourteen she suffered another severe loss. Since then, she's developed a pattern of black
moods and perplexing behavior. Twice in the past she's
made plans to marry, and each time, for reasons no one
could fathom, she broke off the relationship.''

Peri was surprised. ''You mean twice before Harris?''

''Yes, and after the second break-up, she went into the
worst depression yet. That's when Grandmother started
promoting some guy who was in banking. Only then,
Harris came along, and Karen could see no one else. Before, she had been only seeking a means to establish a
new life, but with Harris, you could tell it was true love.
And he felt the same about her. It would have worked, I
know it.'' His tone was bleak. ''Yet now, you say she's
broken off with him, too. It can only mean she's heading for another emotional tailspin.''

Moved by his concern, Peri sympathetically touched
his arm. ''Look, this fuss between them is probably minor. A lover's quarrel. Give them time, and—''

Marc interrupted with an unpleasant laugh. ''Give
them time? What, with you around?'' He had slipped
back into his antagonism as if it were a cloak. ''My sister is a lovely young woman, Miss Brendan, but she can't
compete with the kind of distraction you offer.''

Peri received a perverse sense of pleasure from his in-
direct compliment, yet was infuriated to hear it so twisted

against her. "Have we returned to that? I told you—
Harris and I haven't seen each other since we were practically children."

Marc's deliberately scornful gaze roved over her as if
she were for sale. "Well, if he liked you then, it can't begin to compare with the charms you present to him now.
I had the opportunity to examine you by daylight, remember? I don't know why my grandmother feels enti-
tled to interfere, but she obviously thinks her banker
candidate will still have a chance with Karen if you lure
Harris away."

"For heaven's sake, will you listen?" Peri suddenly
found herself near tears. "Maybe you're right about your
grandmother, I don't know. But even if she plotted to use
me as you think, she didn't tell me, so stop badgering!"

The desperate emotion trembling in her voice gave
Marc pause. He studied her, then grudgingly admitted,
"I suppose that's possible. Grandmother didn't achieve
what she has in business by always placing her cards face
up." Stroking his jaw, he finally nodded. "Okay, maybe
you didn't know."

"Thanks for the vote of confidence." She tried to
sound snappy, only to her dismay, she found herself even
closer to tears. The strains of the day, capped by this
dreadfully unfair confrontation, had pushed her to the
brink of exhaustion. Closing her eyes, she drew a deep
breath, trying to summon her remaining strength.

From overhead came the sound of the wind shuffling
through the palm fronds. A night bird trilled a short
burst of melody, the music soaring above the deep
rhythm of waves on the nearby beach. She didn't realize
she had swayed until she felt Marc's hands upon her
arms, warm through the fabric of her blouse.

"Say, now..." His tone was unexpectedly gentle. "I guess it's been quite a day for you, hasn't it?"

"It certainly has." She strove for spirit, but couldn't bring it off. Eyes still closed, it drifted through her head that if Marc were only someone else, she could just collapse against him. He would hold her close and she could sob out all the hurt confusion that had spoiled this last hour of her arrival in Veracruz. Almost in a dreamlike state, she was tempted to give in to this fancy.

Suddenly shocked at her thoughts, she opened her eyes, shaking her head violently. "Look," she said, stepping back, miraculously able to interject crispness into her tone. "Now that we're agreed I'm not plotting against Karen, how do we straighten out this mix-up—this false impression you've given about us having known one another before?"

The moonlight illuminated a devilish upward lift of his mouth. "You mean about us being lovers?"

"Lovers?" She was horrified. "They don't think that!"

He grinned. "They certainly do. Didn't you see it in Harris's expression, or hear it in Karen's giggle? All of them, Josepha and Theo included, think they understand perfectly."

"Well... Well then—" she sputtered, turning toward the villa "—then it's time someone explained the truth!"

"No, you don't." He quickly stepped in front of her and gripped her shoulders. "I'm quite content to have them believe we're entangled. It will show Harris you're strictly off limits." His voice dropped to an ominous note. "And if you're truly innocent of my grandmother's scheme, you'll be happy to go along with me for Karen's sake. Despite her smiles and dimples, she's a troubled young lady and I won't allow her to be hurt."

"Please..." His fierce determination alarmed her as much as his forceful grip. "Please, you're hurting me."

"I'm sorry." He dropped his hands, but not his intensity. "I need your help. Will you agree?"

When she hesitated, he reasoned in a softer tone, "If Harris means nothing to you, I'm actually asking very little. Just pretend we met back home. A few dinner dates, the theater, a few parties..." She had been rubbing her shoulders, and he moved her hands aside, lightly caressing her bruised flesh with fingers that now were gentle. "Besides," he murmured in a husky voice, "will it be so dreadful to pretend my attentions are welcome?"

Jerking free, she glared at him, trying to hide the fact that she was trembling. "All right! For Karen's sake, I'll go along with your plan. But that certainly doesn't allow you to...to..." She groped for the word she wanted.

"To take *liberties*?" he supplied with a soft chuckle, flashing his winning smile.

The look of him, so arrogantly sure of his appeal, made her boil. "It doesn't allow you to touch me, is what I mean," she ruled, eyes flaming. "Karen has already informed me of your...of your *goatish* reputation, so don't bother wasting your well-practiced techniques. It just so happens you're a shining example of the cheap, shallow type of man I loathe."

"My, my," he responded serenely, as if misreading her insults as compliments. "Then you don't have to worry that anyone will expect our little fling to become serious. Cheaply and shallowly, I flit from flower to flower. When your stay here is over, we'll bid each other farewell and that will be the end of it for both of us."

"And not a moment too soon, I assure you!" Hadn't some instinct warned her against him from the start? Oh, how right she had been.

He chuckled. "At least this will number among one of my more unusual affairs."

"I would appreciate you not using that word."

"What word—affair? My, aren't we prim and proper. But, if you already know my reputation—*goatish*, I believe you termed it—you know that won't wash. I would hardly stay intrigued with a girl who kept saying no, would I?" He lifted a speculative brow. "And to be honest, you don't look like a girl who would keep saying it. Not with those voluptuous curves and those full lips, as ripe and sweet as country plums."

Speechless with fury, she lifted a hand to strike him, but laughing, he caught her wrist. "Simmer down, Miss Brendan." He obviously was enjoying himself. "Truce, all right? Best cool that temper, because it's time we rejoined the others."

His words alarmed her. Exhaustion had robbed her of poise or ingenuity: how could she face the others playing the game he had forced her into? "But I can't," she cried, beginning to fall apart. "I can't go back in there now. What will I say? About us, I mean. If Karen asks questions about us, what will I tell her?"

"You're a bright girl," he chuckled with confidence. "You'll think of something." Slipping an arm around her, he directed her toward the lounge. When she hesitated, he slanted a mischievous look down into her eyes. "Come along, or do you want them to speculate we've tarried because I'm out here making leisurely love to you on the grass?"

Exasperated to the point of inarticulate sputtering, she clenched her hands. "You . . . you . . ."

"Cad?" he suggested helpfully. "Bastard? Vile worm?"

"All three of the above!" she snapped, shaking loose from him and marching on ahead.

Chapter Three

In the morning, Peri awoke feeling rested and refreshed. Remembering the previous evening, she couldn't suppress a reluctant appreciation for how smoothly Marc had managed when they returned to the lounge. Instead of leaving her floundering, he had skillfully taken charge, manipulating the conversation so that Josepha was led into observing that the hour was late and that their guest must be tired. Peri had then been able to gracefully escape to her room. Regardless of her personal feelings, she could see that Marc had qualities that probably made him extremely valuable to Estelle in business.

Thoughts of her employer made her ponder Marc's suspicions anew. Thinking back, it became apparent that on the day she had seen him in the store, he and his grandmother must have discussed Karen. Peri wondered if Estelle had truly sent her to Veracruz with the secret hope that she and Harris might share an attraction. There was no way to be sure.

Frowning, she considered her bargain with Marc. He made it sound so simple—she need only pretend they had shared a few enjoyable moments back in the States. Then she remembered his smile when saying that people would assume they were having an affair. Suave confidence had seemed to radiate from his every pore. God, how she hated that sort of man. So arrogant, so smug about his masculine prowess. She remembered the steel of his arms and the unyielding strength of his body as he crushed her against him. Her tongue explored her lower lip, which felt swollen and tender. He hadn't even bothered to apologize for kissing her so forcefully. Did he think she took pleasure in being helplessly overpowered? Probably. He probably assumed there wasn't a woman in the world who would spurn him.

Thrown into turmoil by her thoughts, she arose. Dressed in a coral-pink nightgown that heightened the fair fragility of her complexion, she padded to the window and parted the draperies to golden sunlight and a pine-scented breeze. She leaned out the open casement, feeling soothed. A bird darted by, and from the red-tiled eaves came the trilling call of its mate. Looking beyond the palms and evergreens that stood between the villa and the shore, she saw the limpid jade of the gulf spilling out endlessly until becoming one with the horizon. A sailboat at anchor bobbed jauntily, the mast catching the light like a silver spear. She wondered if the boat belonged to Marc.

Karen's cheerful call sounded at the door and Peri called back that it was open.

Bounding in, Karen exclaimed without preliminary, "I'm still reeling! To think you and Marc already knew one another, only you didn't know it. Didn't know he was Marc Raymond, I mean." Apple-cheeked face gleaming from a morning scrub, she flopped on Peri's bed.

"I knew his name of course," answered Peri, having decided how to handle the situation. "What I didn't know was his relation to my big boss." Slipping into bra and panties, she took nile-green slacks and a matching top from a drawer. "If he had been aware your grandmother had hired me to come here, he probably would have explained the connection, but since we hadn't seen each other for several weeks, the subject never had a chance to come up."

"Whoa!" Karen was frowning. "What do you mean you hadn't seen him? I thought you were especially good friends."

Delighted with how Karen was taking the bait, Peri hid a satisfied smile. "Oh, no. It's been a casual thing. We've only dated a few times." Buttoning her blouse, she looked at herself in the mirror rather than facing Karen. "He's terribly attractive, just as you said, only as you well know, he's hardly interested in a girl with a career on her mind instead of romance."

Chewing on the red ribbon that tipped her thick braid, Karen asked, "But you do like him, don't you? Last evening, the way you greeted one another, I assumed..." Her voice trailed off.

"Oh, I can imagine what you thought," laughed Peri. "What everyone thought! That certainly was an exuberant welcome he gave me, but that's Marc, right? It doesn't mean a thing and both he and I know it."

Running a brush through her apricot-colored curls, Peri was certain she had scotched any thought of a serious relationship between herself and Marc. Then, honoring her promise to make it clear she had no designs on Harris, she turned, adding brightly, "But I'm terribly glad Marc's here, you know. I can't think of better company for a stay at a luxurious villa than your charming brother.''

Karen sighed happily. "Marc *is* a lot of fun, isn't he?''

Peri noticed that the girl seemed relieved to hear her praise Marc. Was it because Karen couldn't imagine her not finding him irresistible, or because it indicated she wasn't interested in Harris? After all, Karen wouldn't be the first female to keep a jealous eye on a man even after throwing him over.

Downstairs, a serving girl, Margarit, announced that they were the last to eat: everyone else had finished and gone into town for one reason or the other. Peri had mixed feelings about Marc's absence. She knew she should feel relieved to be spared his odious company, yet she was vaguely disappointed. She decided it was because she had wanted to demonstrate her self-composure. Unlike the previous evening, she wouldn't let him catch her at a disadvantage again.

Breakfast was served in an outdoor courtyard where white Moorish arches framed the swimming pool. Stone urns held the largest geranium plants Peri had ever seen— small shrubs, actually, the profusion of their scarlet blooms vivid against the green-blue of the water beyond.

Luis, wearing jeans and a plain T-shirt, appeared with coffee, a food tray and a cheerful grin.

"No messages today?'' inquired Peri, scribbling imaginary designs on the air in front of his chest.

Understanding her meaning, he laughed, black eyes shiny as berries. "Not today *señorita*, but Señor Marc has given me many. One shirt says I'm With Stupid. I like best to wear it when I'm with my cousin, Carlos, who thinks he's so smart because he's the oldest.'' Eagerly, he turned to Karen. "I have seen Señor Marc's boat, but I haven't seen him. Do you think he brought me another funny shirt?"

"You'll have to ask him yourself," answered Karen. Looking up from the melon she was eating, she teased, "To be fair, it's time Carlos got a shirt so he can defend himself."

The idea appealed to the boy. "You are right! Carlos should, how you say, get even? But what words should be on his shirt?" He looked expectantly from Karen to Peri.

Peri wrinkled her nose thoughtfully. "How about My Cousin Stole My Shirt?"

Luis pondered a moment, then exploded into giggles. "Yes, very good! For him to wear when I wear my Stupid shirt. Two insults against me, yes? I am not only the stupid one, I am also a thief! I will ask Señor Marc if he can find such a shirt." Face alight with this plan, the boy skipped off.

"What a darling!" laughed Karen.

"He certainly is," agreed Peri. "Do his parents work here, too?"

"No, he lives here with Concepcion. His parents are farther north, in a village near Poza Rica. That's close to the ruins of El Tajin, the place Aunt Josepha and Uncle Theo talked about last night. When they take their trip there, Luis will go along and visit his family."

Peri sipped coffee that had been delicately blended with chocolate and spices. "Why is he here if his parents are both living?"

"They don't get along. With all the quarreling, Concepcion thought it best to have the boy with her."

"Speaking of quarrels . . ." Wondering if she might be walking on thin ice, Peri nevertheless forged ahead. She'd heard Marc's version of Karen's disastrous love life and now wanted to hear what the girl had to say for herself. "Didn't you tell me yesterday you'd just ended a romance? If you don't want to talk about it, okay, but Marc indicated that the man involved was Harris."

Karen shrugged, her manner breezy. "Harris and I had a brief infatuation, but now it's over. I suspect I got bored with him. Like Marc, I'm fickle."

Peri was troubled. For an instant she had glimpsed a pained expression in Karen's eyes that didn't match her frivolous pose. But, if neither Karen nor Harris were happy over breaking up, why had they allowed it to happen? Peri recalled Marc saying that Karen's emotional problems had begun after suffering a bad loss when she was younger. He hadn't said what the loss had been. Did the secret to her present behavior lie in the past? Peri was curious, but intuitively felt it would be best not to question Karen herself.

When breakfast was over, Karen jumped to her feet. "Let me show you the work Estelle's having done on the south wing. Since Margarit says Harris and the work crew have gone off for supplies, it will be a good time to look without being in their way."

Peri wagged a finger. "I'd love to, but not now. This morning, we tackle those photo files, remember?"

"Rats!" grumbled Karen, grinning. "I thought I was going to get away with it. Okay, slave driver, follow me. But don't say you didn't have your chance to escape."

The first signs of the chaos appeared as Karen led the way through her bedroom, which adjoined her work space and darkroom. Biting her lip to restrain comment, Peri couldn't understand how anyone so fresh and pretty could hatch from so untidy a nest. Every door and drawer was opened to spill out clothing, makeup and jewelry. The dressing table, bureaus and chairs were piled high.

"Just as bad in here," announced Karen, sounding almost proud as they proceeded into her jumbled work area.

But, as Peri was soon to discover, even though the photos for the proposed book lay in disorder, the photographs themselves showed thoughtful planning and careful execution.

"These are wonderful!" she acknowledged, looking at shots of stone idols, architectural details and gem-studded silver figures. "Any one of these could be framed as an artwork. But how will you use them in the book? Is there written material to describe the items and to identify the sites where they were found?"

"Sure, I made notes like crazy." Pert as a pixie and eagerly cooperative, Karen unearthed a haphazard collection of notes scribbled on assorted scraps of paper. "For each shot, I made detailed descriptions. All you have to do is read each one, then find the photo that matches it."

"All *we* have to do, you mean," corrected Peri.

In a small voice, Karen said, "Somewhere I have an outline for the entire book. It might help." When Peri remained silent, Karen scrambled to find the outline, which she presented, then stood swaying back and forth from one foot to the other like a little girl who hopes to wheedle out of a scolding.

Heaving a sigh of relief, Peri found that the outline was clear and concise. She closed her eyes in concentration, mentally preparing the best approach to the project. It was rather like fitting together puzzle pieces. At first, she could see nothing except odd, mismatched bits, but then, as her mind played with various possibilities, she saw how the pattern should take form.

"Okay," she said briskly, opening her eyes. "At some future point, this outline will become our bible, but right now, the job will be to gather the photos and arrange them by subject category."

"Will we do the same with my notes?" Karen asked, twisting her braid. She sounded apprehensive, as if confronting a mountain too steep to climb.

"Let's concentrate on one thing at a time. Look ahead too far and you can feel overwhelmed." Peri's tone was patient and she was rewarded by seeing the tension on Karen's face ease.

After Karen had unearthed all the photos, Peri sat on the floor and separated them into two piles. Taking one pile, she patted the floor beside the other and said cheerfully, "Come on, pardner. Get on down here and let's go to work."

By noon, credible progress had been made. Massaging the stiffness at the back of her neck, Peri didn't realize she and Karen were no longer alone until she heard Marc call from the open doorway, "Isn't it time you two took a break?"

"Oh, Marc!" Karen stretched out her arms. "Peri's helping me make sense of this mess in the most wonderful way!" Bubbling with enthusiasm, she showed her brother the results of the morning's labors.

"Very fine indeed," he approved, impressed. His dark, perfectly shaped head bent near his sister's, the clean lines of his profile silhouetted against the bright square of the window. Simply by striding into the room, it seemed to Peri that he had taken command of it, his virile masculinity drawing her eyes against her will. He was dressed in well-cut gray slacks and an ice-blue sport shirt. The attire was ordinary, yet the bearing of his superbly well-conditioned body lent the garments a unique style.

He turned, catching Peri's stare. Color suffused into her face as she realized she was sitting like a supplicant at his feet. Yet, if she got up, that would seem awkward, too.

"I'm seeing a lot of progress in what Karen is showing me, Peri." Honest appreciation and respect ran through the timbre of his deep voice. "Keep her going along like this and the book will become a reality after all."

"We're not thinking that far ahead," interposed Karen. "Although we have the overall goal in mind, we're only concentrating on the task at hand. It keeps things under control."

Marc lifted an eyebrow. "Indeed? That's quite sensible." He shot a quicksilver glance in Peri's direction, acknowledging that she was responsible for Karen's new attitude.

His praise launched the girl into another excited explanation of the work so far. He nodded and smiled, awarding her such single-minded attention that he seemed oblivious to everything else.

Peri watched. At first she was warmed by the interest he was showing his sister, then she became critical. There could be no doubt of his sincere devotion to Karen, but she was willing to bet he used a similar technique on women he considered sexual game, giving each one the impression that she was the only person in the world.

As if her thoughts had been transmitted telepathically, Marc shifted his gaze to her. The dark centers of his eyes looked large and strangely compelling against the gray of his irises. She stared, her heart beginning to beat more rapidly, a tightness choking her throat. Spellbound, she could not break free and it seemed it was the same for him. Abruptly, with a jerk of her head, she tore her eyes away, feeling as breathless as if she had been running.

"It's lunchtime," he said, his voice holding an odd, husky note. He consulted his watch, then took a step, stretching out a hand to assist Peri to her feet. "Concepcion is laying the table downstairs, but I thought we should go out. How does that sound, darling?" His eyes locked upon hers once again.

Flickers of trepidation ran along her skin. Making no move to take his hand, she realized she didn't want to be alone with him. Nervously, she moistened her lips, feeling the lingering, swollen tenderness. "I don't think we should. Not since Concepcion has prepared for us."

"But she hasn't." Smile tantalizing, he bent to remove photos from her lap. "I've already told her we won't be joining the others."

Permitting no further resistance, his large hand was firm and warm as he drew her to her feet. The lids of his eyes narrowed briefly, dark lashes screening a metallic silver-gray. The measured emphasis of his words reminded her of their bargain as he intoned, "They will *expect* us to go out together."

"Yes, I see," she said faintly, realizing she was cornered. Unconsciously seeking a delaying tactic, she glanced at her dust-smudged attire. "I'll have to change."

He nodded. "Meet me in the entry court when you're ready. By the way, a skirt instead of slacks, all right? We'll be going to a village café where women are expected to follow traditional customs."

Irritation tightened the usually gentle curve of Peri's mouth. He had it all programmed, didn't he? Right down to directing her how to dress. He obviously was a devotee of those "traditional customs" himself, expecting meek submission to his orders. Then, with a sigh, she stifled her temper. Why was she getting so upset? It was only lunch, after all. In so small a matter, there seemed little point in trying to oppose him.

Chapter Four

"That blouse is pretty," commented Marc after they were seated in the café.

"Why, thank you." His compliment surprised her because she was willing to swear that something about her appearance had annoyed him when they had met in the entry court. She glanced down at the pastel blue cotton, which had a gathered neckline and ruffled cap sleeves. With it, she wore a navy skirt.

"I've always been told blue is my best color—that it brings out my eyes."

He nodded, studying her with a practiced air. "More so than the green outfit you wore earlier."

She was thoughtful, her mind having drifted back to the past. "Periwinkle blue," she mused. "That's how my father described my eyes."

Marc lifted a dark brow. "Peri Periwinkle?"

She flushed. Unknowingly, he had stumbled upon the pet name her father had given her. It was disconcerting to hear it from the lips of a man who looked nothing at all like Leslie Brendan, yet who reminded her of him in a significantly painful way. She turned her head to survey her surroundings.

She had been enchanted by the café at first sight. Located in a waterfront village south of Veracruz City, it was a thatch-roofed, stucco-walled dollhouse. The waitress knew Marc and had greeted him with coy, flashing eyes that deliberately ignored Peri. Hips swaying, she had led them out to a table on a balcony that overlooked the Jamapa River. The wrought-iron railing was decorated with hanging baskets of begonialike red flowers. A small green parrot in a raffia cage uttered a constant monotone of gravelly sounds as he contentedly preened himself.

The waitress, whom Marc addressed as Delores, continued to simper and flirt as she waited for his order. The menu was handwritten in Spanish, putting Peri at a total disadvantage.

"Order for me, please?" she begged, laughing at her ignorance. "Anything, just as long as it leaves me room for another one of Concepcion's excellent dinners at the villa tonight."

"Anything?" The crevice in his cheek deepened with pleasure. "They do something marvelous with prawns here. Rather like shrimp scampi, only with a difference."

"That sounds perfect." She was amused to see how Marc liked having the reins turned over to him. She had allowed him to tell her what to wear and now she was letting him tell her what to eat. It would probably put a considerable hitch in his stride to know that instead of feeling awestruck, she was simply being generous. Here she was, seated across from what was probably one of the most stunning swashbucklers in the entire western hemisphere, yet she felt as cool as a cucumber. Why had she feared being alone with him? Since she had accepted his invitation, she might as well enjoy herself.

"Tell me about the wing that's being restored," she asked after Delores sashayed off with their order. "From the little I've seen, it appears spacious."

Marc smiled. The light filtering in through the tree branches outside the balcony warmed the metallic quality of his eyes, lending them a hazy softness. "So it is. The villa was built as a hotel, and my grandmother has been thinking of returning it to its original purpose. Josepha and Theo are getting along in years, and there's no telling how long they will want to continue tramping around researching jungle ruins. They've expressed an interest in managing the hotel as a retirement project."

A frown drew Peri's brows together. "But that will force you and other family members to give up your privacy."

"That's where the reconstructed wing comes in. When Harris is finished work, the far end of the villa will be a family compound."

"Oh, I see. Karen was about to give me a tour this morning, only our work came first. By the way—" Peri couldn't suppress an inward smile. "When Karen questioned me about our supposed relationship, I made it clear we're nothing more than *very* casual friends."

Marc pretended dismay. "But fabricating the lurid exploits of our past was to be our main luncheon topic!" His voice dropped to a seductive purr. "Of course, we still must do a little."

"A little what?" She was warned by a suddenly wicked smile that he was setting her up for something.

"A little planning. It wouldn't do for you to claim we were introduced at a party while I said we first met in the park."

She narrowed her eyes, still on guard. "I suppose we could agree on such a harmless detail, not that the question will ever come up."

"One never knows." He lifted his broad shoulders in a debonair shrug. "One should be prepared. Let's agree we were introduced at a party by a mutual friend."

She toyed with a spoon. "That sounds all right, I guess."

"Splendid! So, we were introduced—me the shallow bounder, you the modern working girl." He angled his head, the dappled sunlight picking out chestnut tones in the dark waves. "Next, I had planned for us to decide whether we spent the night after the party at my place or yours, however—" He held up a hand to forestall her blistering objections. "Since you've convinced Karen our friendship is so dull, I guess we have nothing further along that line to discuss."

"You guess exactly right," she replied, thoroughly exasperated by his way of straying into forbidden territory. Delores arrived with the meal and Peri was glad for the distraction.

As they ate, Marc dropped his raillery and turned into a thoroughly pleasant companion. Peri was female enough to especially appreciate being the sole object of his attention while poor Delores was knocking herself out with no result whatsoever. When serving dessert the waitress boldly pressed her hip against his shoulder while reaching across the table. Then, pausing to play with the parrot, she made exaggerated kissing sounds and cooed Spanish words that Peri guessed must be hot-blooded endearments that Marc was supposed to overhear and ponder.

After they finished their leisurely lunch, Marc escorted Peri from the café, leaving a wistful Delores clutching the sterile consolation of a lavish tip. Riding away in the car, thinking how much she had enjoyed herself, Peri suddenly remembered something she wanted to know.

"Marc?"

"Yes?" he asked with a winning lift of his scarred eyebrow.

"Tell me about the loss Karen suffered when she was a teenager. I didn't want to ask her myself, yet—"

The change that came over his face was as swift as the change from day to night.

"How did you know about that?" came his harsh demand.

"You told me yourself." Peri felt she had stepped on a land mine. Any second it would blow and scatter her sky high. "You . . . you said that when Karen was fourteen, she suffered a severe loss that seemed to signal the start of her depressed moods."

Having gone white, he drew his breath through narrowed nostrils. Gaze fixed upon the road, his drawn face emphasized his hawklike profile.

"Yes," he said in terse agreement. "I did tell you that. I had forgotten."

Not knowing what else to do, she blundered on. "So, I was wondering—"

"It's not necessary for you to be concerned. It is, to put it bluntly, none of your business."

"Yes, only—"

"None of your business, Miss Brendan." The look he shot her from beneath glowering brows caused her to flinch. "I shouldn't have made reference to the episode, and it's best erased from your mind. Understood?"

She was struck speechless by his vehemence.

"Is that understood?" he repeated, slowing the car. Later she was able to reason that lifting his foot from the accelerator had been only a reflex action, but at the time it seemed threatening, as if he were preparing to stop and use force if she didn't respond as he wished.

"Of course," she answered, struggling to keep alarm from showing. "If that's what you think best."

"I know it's best." His eyes were frosted granite.

The car resumed normal speed. For the remainder of the return ride, no further words were exchanged.

Karen, clad in an orange bikini, dashed from the front door the moment Marc brought the car to a stop at the villa.

"Oh, I'm so glad you're back!" she cried breathlessly to Peri. "The most awful thing happened! I found another box of photos we'll have to sort."

Marc, who had climbed hurriedly from the car when seeing his sister's whirlwind approach, snorted in disgust. "Lord, gal! The way you came rushing up in your bathing suit, I thought someone had drowned or something."

Karen laughed. "Wow! And I thought I was the one who liked to be dramatic."

"Well, it *was* you," Marc defended, "running up acting so stricken..." He allowed his words to trail off as if realizing any argument would be futile. Peri was pleased to see that for once, he had lost command. She was also grateful when Karen whisked her into the house so fast that there was only an opportunity to call back a thanks to Marc for a luncheon that was, in retrospect, quite a tangle of high and low points.

During the next few days Peri found Marc's behavior pleasantly, but not overly, attentive. She told herself she was relieved that he had apparently given up the supposed heavy romance angle to their relationship. This way, she could focus her attention on Karen, where it belonged.

Apparently delighted to be immersed in her project at last, Karen displayed none of the dark moods Peri had been warned about, nor did she give any indication that Harris had ever meant more to her than a casual acquaintance. Peri noticed, however, that Harris could not look at the girl without his heart in his eyes.

One afternoon later that week, while Karen was catching up on work in her darkroom, Peri was the first to arrive at the pool, the after-siesta gathering spot. Although the sun had passed its height, the weather was sweltering. Taking a chair in the shade, her thoughts drifted unbidden to Marc.

For the most part, she had to admit she found him amusing and charming. Yet, there were moments when she caught him examining her in a way she couldn't define. Did he still suspect her of being in league with his grandmother? Despite his carefree manner, Peri was beginning to see he thought things through very deeply. Disturbed, she realized she was most comfortable when she could think of him as nothing but a handsome, hollow shell of a man.

"So, how is Karen progressing on the book?" demanded Josepha cheerfully, her bawdy voice shattering the sultry hush as she entered the pool area, her brilliantly flowered tent dress billowing around her as she sat down.

Not waiting for a reply, the woman dropped her voice to an uncharacteristic hush. "Karen's dilly-dallying has been an embarrassment. She got the job on her own merits, but the foundation that awarded the grant consists of university people and museum directors that Theo and I have known for years. They can't help wondering why we can't get the kid on the ball, you know?"

Peri nodded reassuringly. "Things are going well. The last of the descriptions has been matched with the photos, and she's ready to start selecting the best ones."

Josepha placed an impulsive hand on Peri's arm. The concerned expression in her slanted eyes reminded Peri very much of Estelle. "Theo and I have been worried about more than the book. When Karen slammed the door on Harris, we feared she would go off the deep end again. I think your presence has helped steady her."

"I'm glad," Peri answered, suddenly thinking that Josepha would be the ideal person to ask about Karen's past. She hadn't promised Marc she would probe no further—only that she would not bring up the subject again with him. A tricky point, and if he found out, he would be furious. She felt a chill as she vividly recalled his manner that day in the car. Did she want to risk his anger?

The decision was taken from her hands when Karen appeared, carrying a tray of refreshments.

Dressed in her bikini, her braid pinned atop her head, she gave a critical glance at Peri's pink shorts and peasant blouse. "Why aren't you in a swimsuit?" She placed a pitcher and glasses on the table. "Gads, what a scorcher! Harris and his crew must be having a rough time if they're trying to get much done today. I'm going for a swim."

With no more ado, she crossed to the edge of the water and jumped in, holding her nose like a child. Surfacing, she asked her aunt, "Where's Uncle Theo?"

"Inside, working out schedules for our trip to El Tajin."

"It's too hot to discuss schedules," announced Marc, appearing in time to overhear his aunt's words. At Peri's chair, he paused to brush his fingertips along her arm. She caught her breath, startled at how her flesh tingled, as if his touch were a feather of fire.

He bent down to speak, his voice a low murmur, but Karen interrupted by splashing water in his direction and calling, "You shouldn't use the hot weather as an excuse to neglect schedules. Peri's been teaching me that consistent planning is the path to success."

Marc laughed, stepping to the pool's edge to flick water with a foot. "Miss Super Organization. There's nothing worse than a new convert."

Karen's reply was to splash more water.

With a tolerant chuckle, Marc retreated to a deck chair, and Peri felt a twinge of disappointment. Whatever he had been about to say to her a few moments ago had apparently all been forgotten as he folded a beach towel into a makeshift pillow and stretched out.

Karen, arms resting on a foam doughnut, floated quietly. Josepha, complaining it was too hot, returned to the house. Except for a faint insect buzz and light shuffling of palm fronds in the breeze, the afternoon held no sound.

Peri shifted so she could see Marc more easily. Naked except for his black swim trunks, he lay relaxed, eyes closed, vulnerable for the moment despite his physical size. A whitened scar along his ribs played up the tanned, well-formed magnificence of his body in much the same manner as the unevenness of his broken nose and marred eyebrow emphasized the handsomeness of his face.

Peri's eyes roamed, traveling down his chest, unconsciously following the pattern of hair that curled crisply, descending in a narrowing line down his flat belly to his swimsuit. Her surreptitious glance moved wantonly downward, lingering here and there, only slowly coming to the long length of his legs and to his feet.

She was startled by the nearby sound of Karen's voice. Belatedly she realized that the girl had left the pool and now stood by the refreshment table. Eyes twinkling, she spoke to Peri.

"We'll have to get you a road map so you can mark special points of interest worth revisiting."

"Karen!" moaned Peri, dismayed that her scrutiny of Marc had been observed.

"What's this?" asked a curious Marc. Eyes heavy-lidded and lazy from drowsing in the sun, he looked at the two women.

"Nothing to do with you, brother dear," Karen lied brightly, pouring glasses of punch to take into the house for her aunt and uncle.

Marc looked quizzically at Peri. "Why do I get the feeling my sister isn't being truthful?"

"Because you're too conceited to believe a conversation can revolve around any topic except you."

Marc's smile came as slow as honey. "You're probably right."

When Karen returned, Harris was with her. He explained, "Even though siesta was over, it was still too hot to work, so I gave my men the afternoon off." His pink forehead was damp with perspiration and the blond beard made him look even hotter. Karen suggested they all swim, but Marc had a different idea.

"Let's row the dinghy out to my boat for a sail. The air is bound to be cooler on the water."

This plan was accepted with enthusiasm and forty minutes later, the four of them were underway on Marc's thirty-foot sloop, the *Hummingbird*. Karen was at the wheel, with Harris, his expression worshipful, close by her side. Peri, her wind-tangled curls shimmering in the glare of the white-hot sun, asked Marc where he had gotten the name for his boat.

He grinned in a sheepish way she hadn't seen before. It made him appear younger and less sophisticated. "One of my first solo boat rides as a kid was on a meandering river with a lot of branches. I got lost, or at least, I thought I was. From Josepha and Theo I had heard that the Aztecs worshipped a hummingbird god who once led them safely through the wilderness. When I saw a familiar landmark, I decided the old Aztec god might have helped me out. Since then, I've named all my boats *Hummingbird*."

Peri smiled, liking to think of Marc as an imaginative little boy. By that time they had moved to stand by the rail, watching the coastline slip along as they sailed past. Marc had topped his bathing trunks with a white knit shirt that made his tan appear almost mahogany by contrast. As he leaned forward, his profile was coin-pure against the cloudless sky. Peri had a sudden urge to reach out and trace that proud, majestic outline that ran from forehead to chin, then down the strong column of his throat.

She forced herself to look away, shaken by the intensity of emotion that had swept through her. She told herself the mood must have been brought on by the exhilaration of the gulf air, which was so sparkling after the stillness that cloaked the inland.

The craft approached the city of Veracruz, which was a shimmering dazzle under the glare of the sun, then swept briskly on past.

"There are no more sights along the coast for awhile now," Marc said abruptly, taking Peri's hand. "Come on and I'll show you the quarters below."

Peri was far more impressed than she had expected to be with the boat's interior. Her only boating experience had been on motor launches, and since the sailing craft was so much smaller than those, she had been prepared for a cramped, crudely outfitted space. Instead, what Marc conducted her to was beautifully appointed despite its snugness.

"So, what do you think of her?" he demanded proudly, his satisfied grin conveying his confidence that no one could consider the boat anything except a slice of paradise.

Tucked to one side was a neat galley with an efficient double sink, stove, oven and refrigerator-freezer. The living-dining area was carpeted in a thick, wine-color nap. A couch, chair and curtains were of an attractive design in soft reds, wine and cream. Brass ornaments and decorative items of native Mexican design embellished the walls of oiled teak.

"It's lovely," she approved, "and larger than I thought. Is there space enough for private quarters?"

"There's a small cabin forward, and a master stateroom aft." His eyes twinkled. "I wondered how long it would be before my fatal charm had you thinking of bed."

More amused than annoyed, Peri nevertheless shot him a baleful look. "That hardly deserves an answer."

He chuckled. Standing with his one arm resting on the railing of the companionway, he looked down at her, his expression mischievous. "Now is the time to reveal another bit of Aztec folklore about the hummingbird. It's an ingredient in love potions. One sip and a woman is rendered blind to all men except one."

"Thanks for the warning. If you ever hand me a drink with feathers in it, I'll use it to water the nearest potted palm."

Although her quip was casual, she was more than aware of the effect of his nearness. Looking up into his lean, tanned face, she felt mesmerized as his teasing look dissolved into one of surprising tenderness. As he leaned closer, she felt the heat from his body and could smell the salty tang of sea spray upon his flesh. Senses whirling, she closed her eyes.

"Pretty Peri," he whispered. His finger stroked the velvet cream of her cheek and down the side of her throat. Her pulse pounded, constricting her chest so she could barely breathe.

His breath was warm and sweet upon her face, then his lips touched her closed eyelids in a light, butterfly caress. "I never apologized for my behavior that first night on the terrace," he murmured. "I was too rough. I hurt you, I know."

"You . . ." She looked at him, feeling dazed. Her emotions were so tremulous she could barely speak. "You bruised my lip."

"That was unforgivable." His fingertip brushed her mouth then slipped to her chin, tilting her face up to his. "I'll kiss it better."

Her violet eyes widened momentarily, as if she were about to protest as his lips claimed hers, then with a sigh, she surrendered, shutting out all sensation except the touch of his mouth upon hers.

His arms went around her, drawing her close. One large, warm hand pressed firmly against her lower back while the other caressed the nape of her neck, fingers toying with the rosy blond ringlets. He treasured her mouth with tender voluptuousness, and under the sweet and gentle insistence of his kiss her lips parted as she felt a desire to answer the passions he was beginning to arouse within her.

His embrace tightened and the pressures of his hard body against hers drew the remaining strength from Peri's limbs. Sagging against him, she was crushed luxuriously, her warmth cradling his male contours.

Even as her arms lifted to mold him closer, a measure of self-reason returned to her. She remembered how she had once taunted him, saying she was immune to his kind of well-practiced skills. Yet what was she doing now except giving in to the very arts she had scorned? Not for a moment did she believe he was capable of feeling true attraction toward her—he was a man who had only a basic animal response to any woman he deemed available.

Placing her palms against his chest, she pushed him away, her voice sounding unnatural as she said, "I think your sister has had enough time alone with Harris, don't you?" Her pulse still leaped wildly and her breath choked in her throat.

He frowned darkly. "Is that what this was? A way to wile away a few moments while we gave them time to be together?"

"Something like that." She had regained a measure of control over her breathing, but was all too aware of the effect of his nearness upon her senses. Retreating a step, she forced a smile. "Fate may have thrown us together and locked us into this ridiculous bargain to protect

Karen, but I have no intention of allowing the situation to get out of hand. I told you from the start—you're not the kind of man I'm interested in."

His scarred eyebrow hooked upward. "Funny. For a moment there, you could have fooled me."

She laughed. "Oh, I'm human enough, if that's what you mean. But I have enough sense to know when to draw the line."

His nostrils flared. "If you were only drawing the line when you pushed me away, why all the panic? Seems to me, your emotions were a bit more involved than you're willing to admit."

She fixed him with a look of scorn. "Panic? Karen was right—you do have your moments of dramatic fancy."

She bounded up the steps of the companionway and he made no effort to call her back.

She emerged on deck to see Karen still at the wheel. Harris had moved to the stern where he morosely stared out over the gulf, his bearded face reflecting misery. The hazel eyes he turned on Peri were as lost and empty as the seaward horizon.

Marc came on deck a moment later, taking charge of the wheel to turn the boat homeward. His features were tense. Peri knew he was angry because of her rebuff, yet she also realized his feelings probably had little to do with her personally. The idea of any female resisting him must have struck quite a blow to his pride. *Good,* she thought. It was about time he started learning a lesson.

Karen, as sprightly as ever, clapped her hands. "The wind will be with us now, Peri. Grab your hat! We're really going to fly."

The sail luffed as it came about and Peri soon saw what Karen meant. As soon as the white billow caught the wind, they began skimming over the turquoise surface of the water as if it were glass. Spray dashed into her face, but despite the sting to her eyes, she was only aware of exhilaration. She wished the ride could last forever, but all too soon they had reached anchorage in the waters before the villa.

Standing by Harris, Peri wordlessly watched as brother and sister took care of the sails. Marc moved with lithe grace, his strong, supple body performing a ballet that perfectly blended function and form.

Peri suddenly realized that depression had replaced her bright mood of moments before. Her smug thoughts about teaching Marc a lesson were only a way of kidding herself. The memory of his kiss lingered as vividly as a scarlet brand. She was vulnerable to him in a way she hadn't suspected, and if she didn't watch out, she might end up getting hurt.

Back on shore at last, the two men pulled the dinghy up on the beach.

"Help me with this," Karen called to Peri, grabbing the gunwale. "The dinghy has to be flipped over so water won't collect if it rains." Then, not waiting for either Peri's help or for the men to be ready, Karen impulsively tried to rock the boat so the momentum would turn it over.

"Watch out—there's a hole there!" Harris called.

Paying no attention, Karen threw her weight against the dinghy and suddenly her feet began to slide into the depression Harris had warned her about. Losing her balance, she stumbled against the dinghy as it rocked back, scraping her shin.

"I've half killed myself," the girl wailed, sinking to the ground, staring at her leg, which was starting to bleed.

Harris, moving his bulky form quickly, knelt beside her. He examined the wound, then said with concern,

"It's nothing serious, hon, but you're going to have a nasty bruise if we don't get ice on it fast."

Marc finished overturning the boat by himself, then looked at his sister's leg. "Harris is right. The sooner you get ice on that, the better."

Ignoring Harris's outstretched hand, she got up on her own, then stumbled toward Marc, who caught her before she fell. Rounded, pixie face contorting, she wailed, "I don't think I can walk! It's really starting to hurt."

"Upsy-daisy then," Marc said, scooping her easily into his arms.

"I'm too heavy to carry!" she squealed.

"Then I'll have Concepcion put you on a diet," he teased, carrying her effortlessly as he started toward the villa.

Harris, standing beside Peri, disgustedly kicked up a spray of sand. "It should have been me she turned to, not her brother."

"I'm sorry," Peri murmured, feeling bad for her old friend.

Harris kicked sand again. "You know, everything was perfect between us until we started planning our wedding. I could sense her drawing away. When I tried to learn what the trouble was, all she did was get more upset. Finally she said she wanted to break up."

The eyes he turned to Peri were bright with unshed tears. "I know she was once in love with me, and despite what she's said, there are times when I swear she still cares. I can tell by the way she looks at me when she thinks I don't notice." He made a hopeless gesture. "And yet, the rest of the time, she tries to act as if I'm almost invisible. There's no way I can understand it."

Chapter Five

At dinner that evening, Peri, dressed in a coral-colored silk blouse and a black skirt striped in shades of melon, coral and peach, was determined to show Marc that the interlude aboard the *Hummingbird* had an impact of zero upon her. Making a special effort to be vivacious, she laughed gaily, tilting her head often, knowing that the lamplight sent off brilliant sparks from the crystal pendants that swung from her earlobes.

Harris was still in his pensive mood of the afternoon, but Karen, who had needed only a small bandage on her injured leg, was lively as always, her giggles a contrast to Josepha's raucous tones and the mild murmur of Theo's smiling comments. Marc seemed his usual self except for the few times when Peri caught him studying her with a wry smile that was impossible to read.

The next morning when Peri was working with Karen, the girl asked abruptly, "What happened yesterday between you and my brother?"

"Nothing happened," Peri protested, but even as she said it, all she could think of was their kiss.

Karen grinned, toying prettily with her braid. "You said there's nothing serious between you two, but I got the distinct feeling last night that there's been a change. You're starting to fall for him, aren't you?"

"Not at all!" Then, realizing she had spoken with too much feeling, Peri moderated her tone. Busily stacking a pile of papers, she explained crisply, "All this atmosphere of palms swaying under a tropic moon is very nice, but don't think I let it affect me. Or rather, don't think I let Marc affect me."

Karen, sitting across the broad worktable from Peri, cupped her chin in a palm. Her eyes held an impish brightness. "Most women wouldn't miss the chance you're throwing away."

"Chance for what?" Peri scoffed. "Soft words and a few kisses? You would be the first one to tell me he hands them out like a salesman at a candy convention."

Karen said nothing more, but as they continued working, Peri's irritation grew. If Karen wanted to dwell on romance, she should concentrate on her own troubles with Harris and leave other people alone.

Several hours later, when Karen realized she needed to replenish some supplies, the two women decided to take a break and go into town. They were heading out the front door when Marc, quickening his long, easy stride, called for them to wait.

Catching up, he said, "If you need something from town, maybe I can save you a trip. One more errand to run will be no problem." His smile was as dazzling as ever.

"Thanks," replied Karen, "but I have to talk to the buyer at the photography shop myself."

"At least ride along with me." Freshly groomed, his dark beard was only a pale blue shadow along his jaw. As he moved closer to Peri, she became aware of the fresh, spicy scent of his after-shave.

Karen's expression was thoughtful. "Would we be gone long? Peri and I were just going to dash in and come right back. We have a lot of work to finish."

Marc winked at Peri. "How did you transform my sister into such an industrious creature when the rest of us failed?" He returned his attention to Karen. "We can leave right now. I'll take the things Aunt Josepha wants mailed to the post office while you and Peri are in the shop."

"Well, that sounds all right, I guess."

"I bet it sounds great to Peri. I don't imagine she's been looking forward to a ride with you."

"What do you mean by that?" demanded Karen, vexed. "I'm a good driver!"

"The way you operate, you would have to be," he answered cheerfully. "You just have a little trick of never looking at the road ahead. It's unnerving."

Karen glared. "I don't go for rides with people who insult me."

"You do when they offer to buy you lunch. And as soon as we finish eating we'll do our errands and return home."

"Sold," capitulated Karen. She pointed a finger at Peri. "Don't you dare let me walk out of that shop without reminding me to buy more print paper, you promise?"

"I promise," Peri answered, thinking that despite her vows to keep on guard with Marc, there was no danger in this jaunt—not with Karen present.

The streets of Veracruz were busy with noonday traffic, the air filled with the scents of carbon monoxide, salt water and fish. Marc parked near the end of the market section close to the strikingly modern lighthouse, which Peri remembered seeing when she first arrived.

Marc shepherded them through the bustling marketplace, past tuneful marimba bands and strolling vendors, and on to an outdoor restaurant. They took seats under a cerulean blue canopy and looked out over the busy waterfront. Even though it was an ordinary weekday, Peri found a festival atmosphere in the scene, an illusion heightened by the brightly hued native costumes worn by many of the market patrons.

Marc, noticing her fascination, said, "Josepha and Theo love this city. They say that anyone sitting along here sees centuries of history parade by in full dress."

Over their meal—a savory assortment of deep-fried sea foods—the three of them laughed and talked without constraint. Then, as they were ordering dessert, Karen yelped and leaped to her feet.

"I think I see some people I know—be back in a flash." She was off and weaving into the crowd almost before Marc and Peri realized what was happening.

He frowned after her disappearing figure. "Now, does that kid want me to order dessert for her, or not?"

"She said something earlier about sherbet."

"Which would be all melted if I order and she doesn't get back right away."

"Well, she—"

Karen reappeared, smiling broadly. "Listen, I've run into some friends and I'm going with them. They'll see that I get to the camera shop, and then bring me home. See you later!" she called over her shoulder and was gone again.

"So much for her new-found devotion to work," Marc said with exasperation.

"Don't be annoyed with her," defended Peri. "We did as much work this morning as I thought we would accomplish all day. She deserves the time off."

Marc studied her, his expression doubtful. For a moment he stroked his lean jaw with a thoughtful hand, then a smile transformed his face.

"Okay, I'll buy it. Who should know better than you? Besides—" He cocked an eyebrow. "Since we both seem to have the afternoon free, when we return to the villa, we'll go for a swim in the gulf. I think you'll find that swimming there is a lot nicer than in the pool."

When she hesitated, he gave her a sidelong smile. "Come on, Miss Brendan. Must I twist your arm? You made yourself quite clear yesterday about drawing the line. All I'm suggesting is an innocent swim." He tilted his head. "They will expect us to take the opportunity to spend time together, right?"

It suddenly seemed to Peri that they were back on their original footing, simply playing a charade for Karen's sake, only this time, on less antagonistic terms. She decided she felt reasonably comfortable with him in such a harmless relationship.

"All right," she agreed, "but don't let our changed plans make you forget about having to stop at the post office."

Teasing glints sparkled from the depths of his gray eyes. He lowered his voice, intoning, "Whenever we're together, thoughts of playing post office are never far from my mind."

"That's truly corny," she complained, making a face. "It's a good thing you never wanted to go into show business as a comedian."

He laughed aloud, his good humor obviously sincere. "You're right." He winked. "Besides, you'd be the first to point out that being a shallow Don Juan takes up enough of my time as it is."

After returning to the villa, Peri pondered only a moment in her room before deciding on a sea-blue maillot instead of her black bikini. The bikini had appeared conventional enough at purchase, but seemed far too daring when she considered Marc's bold gaze. Even the one-piece garment was more revealing than she would have liked under the circumstances.

As she slipped into her terry beach coat she consoled herself with the thought that the cut and fit of her bathing suit wasn't truly crucial. Marc would hardly expect her to appear swaddled from chin to knee like a Victorian girl. It was her manner not her costume that would remind him that the line between them was firmly drawn.

Downstairs, Josepha, who was doing needlepoint in a shady spot near the pool, informed her that Marc had already headed for the beach. Thanking her, Peri crossed to the short flight of steps that led from the pool terrace to the sandy path. She gave a cheery wave to Luis and Carlos, who were busy trimming shrubbery of red and yellow flowering bougainvillea that flanked the terrace wall. They wore matching shirts pictured with Mickey Mouse.

Passing under an archway of palms, she soon reached the white expanse of the shore. Marc was already in the water, halfway out to the *Hummingbird*, which rocked gently at anchor.

The shallow gulf waters shimmered under the sun, showing the pale green radiance of jade. As Peri had noted the day before, instead of the pounding surf she was accustomed to in the waters off the coast of New York and New England, here there was only the soft, rhythmic incoming of wavelets. Froths of foam, like lacy handkerchiefs cast down by coy flirts, marked the high points of recent billows.

Marc called for her to join him. She paused a moment to gaze back at the villa, her slender feet making faint impressions on the damp sand as she turned. She stood at approximately the same vantage point as the artist who had painted the landscape hanging in Estelle Raymond's office. Admiring anew the palm-sheltered, ocher-walled Moorish palace, she was abruptly swept with the sensation of being on the threshold of destiny. Then, as quickly as it had come, the feeling was gone. She shook her head, bemused by her flight of imagination.

Seeing a towel and Marc's sunglasses on the sand in a sheltered, shady pocket near the trees, she cast off her robe, and covered her body with a protective sun lotion. Then, adjusting the combs that secured the saucy blush-gold ringlets high off her neck, she made for the water.

The sea was noticeably warmer that the water of the pool. She waded out until she was waist deep and kept on walking. The gentle waves swirled about her like warm bath water. Never having been a person with the courage to plunge in abruptly, she was thinking that for once she wouldn't have to wince and shudder when immersing herself. Then she realized she didn't seem to be getting in any deeper. She squinted against the sun's glare at Marc. He appeared to be treading water.

She called, "Is there a big drop just ahead, or are you faking it?"

His laughter rang clearly. "Are you accusing me of setting you up for a trap?"

"Let's say I wouldn't be too shocked." Looking over her shoulder toward shore she figured she had come out about twenty yards.

"Well, there's no drop, but you'll find the bottom does start to incline sharply just ahead of you."

Gingerly testing his words, she edged on. Soon finding herself breast deep, she swam a few strokes then let her legs sink downward. Her toes didn't touch, but peering through the crystal depths she saw that her kicking feet were close enough to bottom to stir cloudy puffs of fine, pale sand.

"It's only a little over seven feet here," Marc said reassuringly as she reached him.

"That's more than deep enough, thank you. Don't expect any Esther Williams wonders from me. There's no sense pretending I ever made much progress beyond an inelegant, but serviceable dog paddle."

"You'd have to work hard to be in danger here," came his confident reply as he combed wet hair from his forehead with his fingers. As his well-muscled arm lifted and flexed, the curls of dark hair in his arm pit showed briefly. "Even a nonswimmer could easily return to the shallows by bobbing under a few times and pushing off from the bottom." He shrugged, adding, "It doesn't get deep until the other side of the shark net."

"What!" His seemingly offhand comment about sharks so shocked her that she momentarily stopped treading water. Her chin dipped and he shot out a supporting hand as she started to flail.

She wriggled free, sputtering, "What do you mean, shark net?" Paddling furiously in place, she looked around for tell-tale fins, then cast a stricken glance back toward shore, which now seemed miles distant. The deep blue of her eyes had darkened with alarm. "Sharks really swim around here?"

"They might if we didn't have the net." He was trying not to laugh. "I've always been willing to take my chances, but Estelle had the net installed anyway. She figures we would need it for guests if the villa is used again as a hotel. So you see—you're perfectly safe."

Her glare was rueful. "And you promised you weren't setting me up for a trap. You knew darned well how I'd react to the word shark."

She moved back to where she could touch the bottom. He followed, using a lazy sidestroke. Reaching her, he stood, his expression becoming contrite.

"I couldn't resist a bit of teasing but you weren't badly frightened, were you? You don't strike me as a woman who stands on a chair at the sight of a mouse."

"Mice and sharks are hardly comparable," she retorted, secretly pleased that she didn't appear to be squeamish.

He chuckled. "No, I guess they're not. Still, it would have been too bad if I'd spoiled your swim. You seem to like the gulf better than the pool. You've hardly done more there than get your feet wet."

"I do like this better," she admitted. Reaching up to refasten one of her combs, she became aware he was noticing how her movement lifted the rounded curves of her breasts. Pretending to ignore the direction of his eyes, she continued blandly, "If I'm going to get a sunburn, I want to smell the salt, feel the gulf warmth and see exotic trees swaying on the beach." Finished with her hair, she was unable to resist giving her suit a little tug that further emphasized her cleavage.

He frowned. "With that fair complexion, I suppose you do burn." With reluctance, he had dragged his gaze up to the complexion of her face.

She was amused. "Not any more, thanks to sunscreen products. But you should have seen me as a kid. Every summer, I won the Miss Lobster award, no contest." She studied his Spanish-dark tan. "I suppose you've never gotten a burn in your life."

"Only from love," he quipped.

She angled her head. "And once burned, twice shy?"

"That's right."

Peri was about to rejoin with further bantering, then considered there might have been a grim undertone to his reply. She recalled Karen saying he had once been hurt by romance. The girl had probably only intended to give him a mysterious aura, but suppose there was a scrap of truth to it?

For whatever reason, Marc switched the subject, remarking that he often enjoyed an early run along the beach. "As you say, the scenery makes a difference. When I'm not on vacation, I try to work out in a gym several times a week, but nothing compares to outdoor exercise in a setting like this."

Picking up the thread, Peri told him her formal exercise consisted of a strenuous dance class she took with several friends from the office. From there, the talk drifted harmlessly and pleasantly from subject to subject. They swam some more, then with unspoken agreement, returned to the beach.

Having already unfolded her beach towel, Peri lay stomach down and closed her eyes. The sheltering branches overhead shielded her from the strong sunlight without impeding the breeze that was quickly drying her wet body. Marc stretched face up on his own towel beside her.

After a silent moment, he said, "It looks as if Karen is truly making progress on her book."

"That she is." Shifting, Peri saw his eyes were closed, the shadows of his thick lashes dark against his cheek. Had she not just heard the sound of his voice, she would have assumed he was asleep. After a hesitation, she ventured, "Everyone kept warning me about her depression, but I haven't seen a sign of it."

He grunted. "Nor have I, but for some reason, I can't feel as comfortable about it as I would like."

"Waiting for the ax to fall?"

"Something like that."

Although he had brought it up, his tone now indicated he didn't wish to discuss the matter further, but Peri persisted. "Harris thinks she still cares despite the way she acts toward him. If that's true, it doesn't make much sense."

"Lot's of things in life don't make sense." Abruptly, he lifted himself on an elbow. "Do you realize your legs are in the sun?" He pressed a finger just below the back of her knee. "You're starting to get pink. That sunscreen probably washed off in the water. Did you bring along more in this beach bag?"

She could feel a throb where his finger had pressed. "Yes, I did, but—" She heard him rummaging in her bag and was about to protest, then fell silent. Obviously, he was only switching the subject to avoid further discussion of Karen and Harris. It seemed quite the afternoon for touch-and-go conversations. Well, she wouldn't push further. There was no point in making him angry as she had done that day in the car.

"Ah," he murmured triumphantly, finding the tube of lotion. "'Maximum sun protection,'" he read aloud. "It really works, hmm?"

"Yes, it really works." Starting to sit up, she reached for the tube.

"I'll do it." He was already squeezing the liquid into a palm. "The back of your legs, right?"

She lay down again, both annoyed and amused at his way of taking control. Just the back of her legs...how could she make a fuss about that? She tensed briefly as she felt the coolness of the lotion on the delicate skin behind one knee, then the gentle, teasing touch of slippery fingers.

"I'm sure there's a technique for this," she heard him murmur in a doubtful tone that was surely a joke, because if anyone had mastered the technique of touching female flesh, it was he. Still, there was nothing to object to as his palm slid with smooth impersonality over her calf. She had given permission after all. His touch was gentle and she felt herself relaxing.

"Do soles of the feet burn?" he asked when finished with both legs from knee to ankle.

"I don't know, it's never happened," she answered lazily. "I never thought about it."

He bent one leg up from the knee and brushed grains of sand from her sole. "No sense taking a chance."

She caught her breath as he stroked the sensitive curve of her high-arched foot. She became aware of other sensations curling through her body. She had never thought of her soles and toes as erogenous zones, but they apparently were. She shifted restlessly as he paid careful attention to her other foot. Yes, they certainly were.

"That's enough," she instructed. "I'm sort of ticklish."

Obediently, he returned her foot to the sand, but his next movements, his hands gentle upon the back of her thighs, were no less arousing. Her muscles tensed, then relaxed as she became accustomed to the soothing pressure. She closed her eyes. Applying both lotion-moistened hands to one thigh at a time, he pressed and kneaded. Despite their skilled gentleness, she could feel that his hands were slightly calloused from working on his boat.

"That's not putting on lotion—that's a massage," she told him, not really objecting because the sensations had become so delightful. She sighed from the depths of a delicious lassitude. To open her eyes would take incredible effort and she was beginning to feel utterly boneless.

"The sun is starting to come through the trees at a different angle," he said. "I'd better do your back, too, while I'm at it."

Sitting with one supporting hand in the sand on the far side of her body, he bent over her, applying the ointment with his free hand. Finished, he walked firm but gentle fingers up her spine, then prodded gently around the muscles of her neck, stroked along her shoulders and down the length of her arms. She relaxed further, almost on the verge of sleep.

"Everywhere, your skin is like satin," he murmured, his fingertips now brushing lightly along a sensitive palm.

"That tickles," came her faint protest, her words blurred. She flexed her hand and closed it into a fist, then helplessly, as if under a spell, opened it to his touch again.

"Like satin," he repeated, and his voice had gone husky. It was a danger signal and she knew it, but she somehow couldn't summon the will to break the magic of the moment. Let him think she had drifted off.

His fingers went up her arm again, trailed down her spine and across her lower back, and then started moving softly up along her side. He barely made contact, yet her skin rippled and tingled. The air was suddenly still; she could hear nothing but the sound of Marc's breathing. She realized she was holding her own breath. Remaining motionless, she felt unbidden tensions begin stirring within her.

The soft pads of his fingertips brushed lightly over her ribs, then, even more lightly along the soft curve of her breast plumped out against the towel. Although she gave no outward sign, the sensation vibrated through her like an electric shock. His hand moved on. It was almost as if the sensual caress had been accidental. Then it happened again. He shifted, lowering himself on an elbow, the warmth of his chest against her back. She could feel his breath against the curls at the nape of her neck.

"Peri?" he whispered. "Peri?"

Not responding, she lay almost delirious with the awareness of every nuance as he once again stroked slyly upward along her ribs. Once again his fingers brushed the soft curve. Then lingered. Caressed.

Bending to rest his body against her, mouth near her ear, he murmured, "Peri, I know you're not sleeping."

He kissed her ear then ran the tip of his tongue inside the delicate shell.

Shuddering, she twisted her head, making a sound of complaint, as if just arousing. She moved in the attempt to shrug off his weight.

Chuckling softly, he held her prisoner. "Sweet Peri, playing possum. I knew you were awake all the while."

"I wasn't, but I certainly am now," she fretted, as if annoyed at being disturbed. "How a person can be expected to nap on the beach when someone..." She tried to move a second time. "Get off."

"Awake the whole time, but playing a game," he intoned, not giving her an inch more freedom. "I know women, remember? Your game is called The Innocent Dreamer and it works like this. Peri wants be loved, but something makes her deny it. So she pretends to sleep, while I, unscrupulous cad that I am, have no shame in taking every advantage." As he spoke, his devilish fingers dug into the sand, making a space for him to sweetly capture the treasure of her breast.

"Marc!"

"Shh. You'll awaken Peri if you're not careful." His laugh was punctuated by another kiss near her ear. "Shh. Let Peri sleep. How far will she let me go as long as I let her pretend this is all a lovely dream?"

"Marc!" She was angry now, angry and embarrassed. He was right about her of course, but how could she have let herself be lured into so stupid and so obvious a trap?

Face hot and flushed, she struggled against his pressing weight, and suddenly, she was free. Only then his grip on her shoulder turned her so that although she now faced him, that broad, bronzed chest still pinned her down.

Gasping, she stared in his face, hovering only inches from hers. His eyes twinkled with mischief.

Damn him, she was thinking. If he was going to try to make her admit he had been right about her being awake all the time, she wouldn't. Never in a million years! Then, instead of the teasing gibe she expected, his face softened. His hold on her relaxed, as if he no longer wanted to force himself upon her, not even in jest.

The warm gentleness of his gray eyes astounded her, held her silent with wonder. His expression, instead of being roguish, had become...well, serious. Tenderly, he touched her cheek. It was as if he were just discovering her. He traced the line of her brows with a fingertip, smoothed the tousled curls at her temple.

"So beautiful," he whispered. As if in slow motion, he lowered his lips to hers. In that moment, it would have been impossible for her to do anything except yield. Her pulses leaped. Her mouth was softly plundered as if its ripe readiness were some exotic wine to be savored, lingered over with rich enjoyment. His muscular length moved against her and her senses were flooded with awareness of his heat, of the tantalizing threat of sheathed power. Desire began to blossom from somewhere deep within her.

Then, cold reason intruded. Men who knew women's games as well as he, surely had their own plays. This one was probably called The Sincere Lover.

Softly he said, "I want you Peri, I really do."

His voice was tender, ringing with honesty. It was a terrific act if she could believe it, only she didn't.

Her mood of surrender had shattered completely. With a cryptic smile, she pushed him away and sat up. "You should have taken your chances when I was sleeping."

"Maybe game-playing wasn't what I was after."

"On the contrary, that was it, exactly," she asserted with merry scorn, studying his handsome face, seeing his wounded expression. The Disappointed Rake. Marvelous casting job, she had to admit. She slipped into her beach robe. "It must be tiresome to feel you must constantly prove your prowess even when it's meaningless—especially against such odds."

For an instant he looked confused, as if he suddenly wasn't at all sure about himself or his motives. Then a spark of humor quicksilvered his eyes. "I thought I could whittle down the odds."

"Well, you were wrong, weren't you?"

"Perhaps." And then, that smile. That dazzling sunlit flash. Despite all her knowledge of its practiced insincerity, it somehow shafted straight to her heart.

Dismayed, she realized what she had done. Instead of dampening his interest, she had actually cast a challenge. And unmistakably, he had accepted it.

Chapter Six

On her way to change from her bathing suit, Peri saw that Karen's door was open. Stepping inside, she called the young woman's name.

"In here, working," came Karen's answering call.

Threading her way through the bedroom, Peri frowned at the ever-present disarray. Clothes lay scattered on the unmade bed. There was not a chair one could sit upon without moving things, nor a bureau that showed a clear surface. Peri failed to see why Karen preferred to live like such a squirrel.

"Well, at least the top of your desk is organized," she commented critically as she entered the adjoining work room.

Karen grinned like a Cheshire cat. "I have my better moments."

Peri gasped as she caught sight of the stack of matched photos and text. "You sure do! It looks as if you've done an awful lot of work."

"I have. I've also decided we don't have any choice except to tag along with Aunt Josepha and Uncle Theo on their trip next week to El Tajín. I guess you've heard they're going to show some fellow anthropologists around. The restored ruins there are too spectacular to ignore, but I only have a few photos. And look—they certainly aren't my best."

"I see what you mean," mused Peri, examining the material Karen had pointed out. She was about to ask more questions about the trip, but then, really began to appreciate how much Karen had accomplished. In wonder, she asked, "How did you manage to finish so much?"

"I've been back here almost two hours," Karen boasted, preening, adjusting the pins that held her thick braid of hair in a coronet around her head.

"You couldn't have been! Not unless you practically followed Marc and me home from Veracruz. I thought you intended to spend time with friends."

Karen's grin deepened. "There were no friends. I merely used that as an excuse. After I went to the photography shop, I grabbed a taxi."

Peri made no attempt to hide her surprise. "Why the fancy story?"

"Isn't it obvious? I wanted you and Marc to have some free time together."

Drawing her terry robe close, Peri leaned against the desk and studied the younger woman thoughtfully. "Why would you want that?"

"Because I think you two are right for each other, that's why."

"But, Karen, I explained—"

"Oh, yes, you said neither of you were interested in a serious relationship, but I don't believe it. Where I went wrong was in emphasizing his playboy qualities. I thought they would attract you, but they only put you off. However, when Luis told me you two had gone to the beach together, I figured my new plan was working and you were learning Marc can be a very special guy."

Remembering the interlude on the beach, Peri's lips tightened. "Believe me, Karen, while your brother may be 'special' to you, playboy is the perfect description."

Karen shrugged. "He's not really that way underneath."

"You couldn't prove it by me. What difference does it make to you anyway?" Peri narrowed her eyes suspiciously. The shadows cast by her lashes made them appear a dark violet. "You've been hoping for something serious between us from the start, haven't you?"

Karen's giggle was merry. "Who can blame a girl for wanting her brother to be happy?"

Peri rolled her eyes. "Karen, the only thing that makes a man like Marc happy is variety." An image of her devil-may-care father leaped into her mind and along with it, all the sorrow he had brought. "Believe me, I know."

"But Marc isn't really like that," insisted Karen in earnest. "He only acts that way because he was once badly hurt. He wants to protect himself by never getting involved again." She touched Peri's arm. "You can show him how wrong he is."

Peri detected an undertone in Karen's voice that sounded desperate. She didn't understand it. She also didn't understand why Karen felt she could correctly analyze Marc's motives when her own romantic life was as messed up as—well, as messed up as her bedroom.

"So just how was your dear brother so cruelly hurt?" she demanded sarcastically, prepared to take whatever Karen said with a grain of salt.

"It was all because of Julie."

Peri's laugh was scornful. "And who was Julie? The first girl to call his bluff?"

Karen winced, but when she spoke her voice held only the faintest reprimand. "Julie was Marc's wife, only she died." With remembered anguish, she added, "They were so happy together, and then the tragedy. It was so sad. Oh, Peri, she was a wonderful person."

For a moment, realizing how badly she had blundered, Peri could find no words. At last, she stammered, "I . . . hadn't realized. I'm sorry I sounded flip. I mean, I never realized Marc was capable of being serious about anyone. This Julie—it sounds as if you liked her very much."

"Everyone did. She was so sweet and beautiful." Karen's manner brightened as happier memories returned. "So tiny, like a silver-blond nymph. She had huge, pale green eyes and when she spoke, it was like hearing little bells. And you should have seen how she loved Marc! When he wasn't around, it was as if a light had gone out, but as soon as he was with her again, she glowed. And he felt the same way about her. You can't imagine how caring he was, how attentive. It was wonderful to watch them together. There wasn't a thing Julie wanted that Marc didn't get for her practically before she asked."

Peri had never believed in made-in-heaven romances, and she had a hard time envisioning Marc dancing in attendance. Still, there was no doubt that Karen was honestly reporting what she remembered.

Puzzled, she asked, "This all happened when you still lived with your grandmother?"

"Not really. I mean I was there when Marc and Julie married, but after a while, I moved to their place.

Everything was wonderful between them, but then—"
Her eyes clouded. "Then, everything came to an end."

"What happened?" Peri asked gently.

Karen didn't answer immediately. Her eyes took on an
inward look as she relived the past events. Her complexion had become alarmingly pale, but she got a grip on
herself and said in a choked voice, "It happened in the
middle of the night. Marc had to rush Julie to the hospital in an ambulance. She was pregnant and nobody
knew about it until she suddenly started to hemorrhage.
The emergency surgery failed to save her. Nothing they
did helped." The girl's voice trembled.

"I'll never forget how Marc looked when he came
home. It was as if he had aged ten years. His heart was
broken, Peri, but you could change all that." Karen's
eyes were beseeching. "I know that if you try, you can
make him happy again."

Peri slept poorly that night. There was no doubt in her
mind that Karen was mistaken about Marc. Not about his
adoration for his wife, Julie—she guessed she could believe that. She could also believe that Julie's death had
left him bitterly determined never to give his heart again.
But Karen was wrong in thinking Peri could be the cure.

Once started on the subject, Karen had spoken vol-
umes about Marc's incomparable wife, and if ever there
was a clinging vine, Julie was it. Peri could understand
why the domineering Marc would want an extremely de-
pendent wife, and if he ever found anyone to take Julie's
place, it would be the same kind of woman. Peri was not
that kind and Marc knew it. But for some reason Karen
refused to face the truth. She was setting herself up for a
disappointment, and no matter how hard Peri had tried
to convince her of it, Karen refused to understand.

"I can tell he really likes you, Peri," she had insisted stubbornly. "You don't know him like I do. He's already caught, and just doesn't know it."

"But I don't want to catch him!" Peri had wailed in utter frustration. "He's the last person in the world that I'd choose. Can't you get that through your head?"

But Karen had only winked. "So you say, Peri. You and I both know the way to win a man like Marc is to play hard to get."

Peri remembered how she had finally abandoned the argument as futile. For some reason, Karen was desperate to engineer a romance for her brother—almost as if she felt personally responsible for his happiness.

Concerned, Peri knew that as soon as Karen added the new photos from El Tajin, her book would be done. That would allow her to focus all her energy on her absurd matchmaking. Peri decided that as soon as the project was wrapped up, she would immediately leave Veracruz. Vivid in her mind was the way Marc had kept looking at her that evening during dinner—amused, knowing glances that made her burn with the memory of those moments on the sand. Yes, for Karen's sake as well as her own, she would clear out as soon as possible.

The next morning Peri learned that an early telephone message from Estelle had called Marc to Paris. During his four day absence, a storm struck the gulf area. Fortunately, there was enough warning so that the *Hummingbird* could be moved to a sheltered mooring. The electricity at the villa was cut for hours as wind and rain battered the house, and Harris said it was only luck that kept the roof of the unfinished wing from lifting off.

Karen, cheerful despite the gloom, claimed to find the storm exciting. Between sessions of mopping up rainwater that leaked in around the shuttered windows, she and Peri continued their work by kerosene lamps.

To Peri's relief, nothing more was said about Marc, who didn't return until late Wednesday night. He then slept until noon the next day, not making his appearance until lunchtime.

"So how is my sister, Estelle?" Josepha eagerly demanded as Marc joined the luncheon table.

"In excellent health and as bossy as ever." He unfolded his napkin with a flourish. "Actually, we spent one of our better times together." One dark eyebrow hooked upward as he added in a quizzical tone, "Maybe I should retract the word 'bossy.' It's a bit early to be certain, but it almost seems she's mellowing."

"Don't let her know that's what you're thinking," Josepha ordered with a laugh. "Mellow sounds like 'soft' and Estelle wants to be tough as nails."

Marc grinned. "Still, I believe she's learning to bend a little bit." He took a helping of fish quiche from the platter Concepcion served, then glanced across the table at Harris. "What's this about the storm nearly wrecking the new wing?"

As Harris described the storm's fury, Peri resentfully considered how Marc managed to dominate a setting simply by adding his presence. Amused by something Harris said, he threw back his handsome head and laughed, the sound thrillingly rich and deep. In vain, she sought traces of the poignant sorrow Karen claimed had shaped him. Every fiber of his being seemed to radiate the virile confidence of a man who had never tasted defeat. No wonder he was confident he could draw any woman he desired under his spell. Her gaze shifted to Harris and she felt pity. As usual, Karen's attention was all on her brother without even a glance to spare for the man she had once planned to marry.

Theo spoke up in his mild fashion. "Marc, on the subject of this storm—your friend Felix telephoned from Mexico City this morning while you were still asleep. He's been informed that a window in his beach house appears broken. He wonders if you can do him a favor and check for possible damage."

"Poor Felix," mourned Karen. "He might have an awful mess. Peri can tell you how the rain beat in around our windows here. If glass is out, Felix probably has a regular flood inside. Let's forget siesta and go over as soon as we finish lunch."

March shook his head. "I can't go until later. I have work to do and phone calls to make."

Eagerly, Harris volunteered, "I'll go with you, Karen." His wholesome, bearded face was alive with anticipation. "My men can work independently this afternoon. You're right in thinking that any water should be cleaned up at once. And the window should be made secure."

Marc glanced meaningfully at Peri and she read his message loud and clear: *Do anything to encourage Karen to be with Harris.*

"That's a good idea, Karen," she quickly agreed. The girl hesitated. Secretly intending to keep in the background, Peri added, "I'll come and help, too."

Not persuaded, Karen pouted. "Felix is more your friend, Marc. You're the one he trusted with the extra key. We should wait until you can come."

"Tell you what," Marc promised, "you go ahead and I'll catch up as soon as possible."

With an air of resignation, Karen agreed, and by the time they were ready to go, the work party also included Luis and Carlos.

They started off, Karen and Peri riding sedately with Harris in the cab of his pickup truck, while in the open back, the two youths reveled as the breeze whipped color into their dark-skinned faces and wildly blew back their coarse black hair.

Felix's house proved to be a stone and stucco cottage directly on the beach south of the villa. It was simple yet charming, with a pink roof and a moon gate in the garden wall. The front of the house faced the open beach while the sides and backyard were thickly planted with coconut trees.

It was the dining room window that was broken. Going inside, the group found that a loose tile from the roof had sailed through the glass, knocked down a curtain and crashed into a china cupboard. By some miracle, only two of the overturned goblets in the cupboard were actually broken, while the curtain, which lay in a rain puddle, was untorn.

While Harris and the boys boarded the window, Peri and Karen cleared up the broken glass and washed the curtain.

"As hot as the sun is, this thin fabric should be dry by the time the work is done," Karen said, leading Peri to a clothesline in the back yard.

The two women then strolled down to the beach. Karen fell into a sulky mood because Marc had failed to arrive. With regret, Peri thought that any idea about throwing her and Harris together for the afternoon had failed miserably.

Still grumbling, Karen looked at her watch. "We'll be ready to leave by the time he shows up."

"It's not as if we needed him," Peri pointed out sensibly.

By the time they returned to the cottage, Harris and the boys were finished and returning their tools to the truck.

"We'd better not forget that curtain," Peri reminded.

Mercurial as always, Karen's grumpiness vanished in an instant. "Hey, right!" She made an exaggerated gesture of jogging her memory. "Why don't you get it while I leave a note for Felix."

To Peri's satisfaction, the curtain had dried without a wrinkle. As she took it down, she pondered how Karen's emotions could swing so quickly from one extreme to another. The girl really was a character. Then Peri heard the truck engine. She didn't think anything of it, until, incredibly, she heard it drive off. For a moment, she stood stock-still, thinking Harris must only be turning around. But no—the truck was definitely leaving.

In disbelief, she ran out through the moon gate and saw the truck bouncing up the shell driveway and turning onto the main road. She could see both Harris and Karen in the cab. Luis and Carlos waved gleefully from the open back. Then they were out of sight.

More baffled than anything else, Peri returned to the house. She still couldn't believe she had been left behind. There on the table she saw Karen's hastily scribbled note and the house keys. But instead of the note being for Felix, it was for her.

Dear Peri, Don't be mad, but it seemed mean to have Marc come out here for nothing. I can't think of anything nicer for him to find when he arrives than you.

Love and kisses, K.

The reason behind Karen's startling change of mood was suddenly clear. Oh, that deceptive, apple-cheeked innocence! Irritated, Peri tore the note and threw it into the trash. Glaring at the keys, she decided she would simply lock the house and start walking. She wasn't far from the villa, and who knew when Marc would arrive? With luck, she would reach the villa before he even left, and so much for Karen's trickery.

Having decided to visit the bathroom, she was still inside the house when a vehicle pulled up outside. It was Marc, at the wheel of a jeep. She finished combing her hair and met him at the door, keys in her hand. Flatly she announced, "I was just leaving."

A brilliant shaft of sunshine coming through the trees high-lighted his cheekbones and the arrogant curve of his nose. "Oh, really? I met Karen and Harris on the road and she told me you were waiting."

Something about the cocksure tilt to his smile told Peri he didn't believe she had really intended to leave, but she ignored it, saying, "Well, you've at least saved me a walk."

He grinned. "Good thing. If I had met you on the road, it would have been too bad. I never pick up hitch-hikers."

"I would have thought you more adventurous than that," she chided as he took the key from her and attended to the door.

"How can you say such a thing, Miss Brendan? You of all people know how conservative I am."

As he spoke he took her arm, leading her to the jeep. Once again, she reluctantly admired how he simply took charge of situations, as if the only right way to proceed was his way. Such confidence must be an invaluable aid to business, only what did that have to do with how her skin tingled at his slightest touch? Annoyed with her susceptibility, she freed her arm.

As he took his place in the driver's seat, he said, "I hope you don't mind a jaunt just before we go back to the villa. Harris gave me the measurements for the window because I want to fetch the glass. Felix is quite a handyman, and will be eager to install it when he returns. He's done me some favors, so I figured it wouldn't hurt to have the glass all ready and waiting."

Assuming she would agree—what woman refused the wishes of Marc Raymond?—he started off.

It took longer to get the glass than either of them had expected, and afterward, Marc, at his charming best, decided they should stop somewhere for dinner.

"But I'm hardly presentable," Peri argued, indicating her jeans and sleeveless blouse. "I thought you had this thing about not shocking the natives with the fashion of American females."

He chuckled. "If anyone asks, I'll explain in my impeccable Spanish that you're a hitchhiker tourist I picked up."

"I thought you didn't do that."

"Tell lies? I do it all the time."

"No. Pick up hitchhikers."

His grin cut a deep crevice in his cheek. "Actually, I pick up good-looking ones whenever I can."

As she soon discovered, the place he took her to was hardly formal.

"I want to show you some native color," he explained as he left the main road for a riverfront village, where there was no bridge and all traffic had to be ferried across a wide strip of swiftly moving muddy brown water.

The scene somehow managed to look picturesque even though the community was little more than a grubby assortment of shacks lining a stony beach where velvet-eyed children capered. The main business was catering to the needs of travelers waiting for the ferry. A mouth-watering aroma of frying food wafted from clustered shrimp stands. The largest stand had an extended porch roofed in tin that was patched with old Pepsi-Cola signs. Under this shade, men wearing broad-brimmed straw hats and native shirts drank milk from whole coconuts that had had their tops hacked open with a machete.

Marc bought tin plates of hot rice and shrimp, and when Peri declined the coconut milk, he got her a bottle of orange drink, the only soda available despite all the cola signs.

Sitting in the parked jeep, they ate their impromptu and surprisingly delicious picnic supper and watched the sun sink in crimson splendor behind the trees on the other side of the river. Several children came around and Peri realized Marc must know them. He talked to them awhile in Spanish, making them giggle, then gave them a few coins before they scampered away.

When Marc returned the plates to the food stand, he remarked whimsically, "Just like returning trays at McDonalds." He directed Peri to an outdoor water spigot where she could wash her hands, then lent her his handkerchief to dry them.

His ease in the unsophisticated native atmosphere showed a side of him that Peri hadn't known existed. During the afternoon, he had been entertaining, interesting, and he had made her laugh. Relaxed, she considered the pleasures of his company. She realized there had been other times when she could say the same—times when she had been able to totally forget the kind of man he represented.

It was twilight when they returned to the beach cottage. Peri held the door while Marc carefully carried in the pane of glass and leaned it against a wall in the dining room.

"There!" he said with satisfaction, rubbing his hands. "Felix will be pleased." He turned to a cabinet and knelt to open a door. "And now, our reward." He pulled out a bottle of coffee liqueur.

Peri demurred, "Oh, but I don't think—"

"Not to your taste?" he interrupted, deliberately misunderstanding. Getting up, he angled aside so she could approach the well-stocked cabinet. "Come select your own."

"No, that's fine. It's just that I thought we should be getting back to the villa. Karen will—"

"Karen will be expecting us whenever she sees us," he interrupted. "She knows we're together."

Peri's reply was rueful, "Oh yes, she knows that all right."

Marc, taking small tulip-shaped glasses from the china cupboard and filling them to three-quarters, gave her a look. "You certainly used an intriguing tone when saying that. Does it mean anything special?"

Peri decided to take the bull by the horns. "What it means is that your sister refuses to believe we're only friends. She fancies herself a Cupid."

His eyes crinkled a moment, as if he felt sure of the game she played. "Well then, it certainly was nice of you to humor her."

"What do you mean?"

"Why, the way you volunteered to stay behind and wait for me this afternoon. It wasn't to be alone with me, oh, no! It was just to make my little sister happy."

Letting him see she was annoyed, Peri tugged at her tangle of apricot curls. "It wasn't my idea. Karen tricked me."

"The plot thickens," he intoned with cheerful disbelief. Handing her a drink, he touched her elbow, guiding her into the living room. It was a square area made more interesting by a mirrored wall and a large, hand-carved screen standing in one corner. He switched on a table lamp and indicated the bamboo-frame couch that had plump cushions upholstered in a colorful jungle print. "We might as well be comfortable while you explain the whole story."

"I know you won't believe me," she huffed in exasperation as she joined him on the couch. "What happened was, while I went to the back yard for a curtain we had washed, the truck simply drove off and left me! Then I found Karen's note and understood it was a set-up."

"Ah, the note." Marc gave his head a sagelike nod, the lamplight hooding his eyes mysteriously. "The proof. The evidence of this monstrous trick."

She saw he still didn't believe her, but somehow the situation had started to become comical. "Yes, oh great detective. The evidence. The problem is, I was so angry, I ripped up the note."

His eyes widened in mock dismay. "You've destroyed your only defense?"

"The pieces are still in the trash."

"But like confetti, I suppose. Impossible to fit back together."

She took a sip of her drink. "No, I don't think it would be all that difficult. We can look if you really want proof. But—" She started to giggle. "Don't you see how asinine this is?" Her eyes sparkled like star sapphires. "There we were, struggling to get Karen and Harris together—which didn't work, by the way—while she was busy hatching romantic plots of her own."

His dark brows drew together. "You're serious, aren't you? I mean, she really did trick you into staying."

She couldn't help laughing. "Sorry if it's a blow to your ego, but that's exactly what happened. Scout's honor."

"Hmm." Finishing the liqueur, he toyed with the tiny glass that looked ridiculously fragile when compared with the lean and sinewy strength of his hands. "My ego will survive, but I *am* disappointed." Then he smiled, that fabulous smile that had never yet failed to take her breath away.

The atmosphere between them seemed suddenly charged with physical awareness. Feeling an urgent need to put distance between them, Peri got up with the pretext of returning her empty glass to the dining room. She then remained standing instead of returning to the comfort of the couch and the danger of his nearness.

Struggling to maintain control over her rampant emotions, she said unevenly, "Marc, I've made a joke of it, but you've got to understand this is serious to Karen. I'm afraid it's going to be an awful blow when I leave and she realizes there's nothing between us and never will be."

Lounging back, long legs outstretched, he studied her, his face revealing nothing of his thoughts. He appeared relaxed, yet the watchful alertness of a predatory animal seemed to radiate from him.

"When are you leaving?" came his question at last.

Defensively, she crossed her arms over her breasts. "The moment the book is finished. All Karen needs are more photos of the ruins at El Tajin. By the time they're printed, everything else should be ready for publication."

"The trip starts the day after tomorrow?"

"Yes."

"And you're going, too?"

"I suppose." She moistened her lips. "I think that's what Karen expects."

His eyes never left hers. "I told Josepha and Theo I might go along. It's a location that's always fascinated me."

A new thought seemed to come to him, and for a moment the tension between them was broken. "Any idea why Karen is so fixed on this idea of the two of us? Could it have anything to do with Harris? I might as well admit I've learned that Estelle didn't send you to lure him away. But could Karen have the same false idea as I did?"

At ease once again, Peri lifted her brow. "Did I hear an apology buried somewhere in all that?"

He had the grace to look contrite. "Yes, I guess so."

"Well, I'm glad I'm off the hook as the resident Jezebel, but Karen isn't throwing me at you to protect her interest in Harris. As far as I can see, she thinks of him as a total nonperson. She just wants you happy and thinks that means finding you the right woman."

He angled his head, studying Peri intently. "And she thinks you might be the one?"

Peri flushed. "I guess I'm simply handy."

His smile was lazy but his gaze was frankly sensual. "Not so handy," he purred. "Not when you're standing all the way over there."

A snappy comeback trembled on the tip of her tongue, but no words emerged. Once again, the atmosphere between them had changed, and this time, so swiftly it left her dizzied. Her pulse started to race. She met his eyes, becoming lost in the compelling depths of endless gray.

The silence stretched into an unbearably taut and endless moment and then, he extended his hand. Eyes still locked upon his, she moved slowly toward him.

Chapter Seven

It seemed to Peri that she simply melted into Marc's arms. With supple ease he reclined upon the long, generous expanse of the couch, taking her with him so that she lay with her weight mostly upon his body, her breasts softly against his chest, one jean-clad leg resting between the two of his. The superior position gave her a satisfying impression of dominance. Even when he laced his strong fingers through her hair and drew her head down so that he could find her lips, she still maintained the feeling of control, as if she were the aggressor, not he.

It was an illusion that was furthered by the almost tentative quality of his kiss, his mouth tender under hers. He caressed her gently, then his hands lay quiet, one curving around her hip, the other upon her back.

His passivity encouraged her to be bold, to hitch her body upward so that she reclined more comfortably against him. Meeting his lips with greater ease, they were joined in a kiss that seemed to go on and on.

Finally, breathlessly, she gasped, "This is hardly the way to convince Karen how wrong she is about us."

His eyes twinkled. "It's convincing me. Obviously, we're mismatched."

She giggled. "Obviously."

Being snugly dressed in shirt and jeans protected her from the vulnerability she had experienced with him on the beach. So what if it was impossible to have a valid relationship with such a man? That didn't mean she had to shy off like a startled rabbit every time he gave her a look. She need only think of the hours they had just spent together to know he could be thoroughly likable. Besides, she enjoyed kissing him, no doubt about it.

"Practice, that's what you have," she said, surprising herself by speaking her thoughts aloud.

"Practice in what?"

Her boldness did not desert her. "In kissing. In making love."

His chuckle was soft. "Practice is what makes it perfect."

"That's what your kind always thinks," she scolded, sliding to lay beside him on the couch. She propped herself on an elbow as he turned toward her, their bodies still closely aligned. His face was level with hers and only inches away as she continued, "What you don't understand is what makes love perfect is *caring*."

He lifted one dark eyebrow in question, his breath lightly fanning her cheek as he spoke. "So, the only thing that rates in your book is what's called 'meaningful encounters'?"

"Exactly."

He looked thoughtful. "Suppose I tell you that every one of my encounters has been meaningful."

She sniffed. "That's impossible."

He seemed increasingly interested. "Don't be too hasty." His one hand remained upon her hip when she shifted position, and now it moved almost imperceptibly over the rounded curve. "Perhaps I have depths you've yet to discover. An ordinary fellow might only be capable of really *caring* only once or twice in a lifetime, but why hold his inadequacy against me?" He caressed her in a way that seemed almost absentminded. "I think I should be judged solely on my own merits."

She couldn't help laughing. "That's what I've done."

"Somehow, you've been misled. Does this book of yours have rules? Like, five encounters can be meaningful, but more is stretching the limits?"

"I would think five is already too much."

"How about three?"

"That sounds about right."

He chuckled softly and she felt the vibrations from his chest. "That tells me you've fallen madly in love a maximum of three times."

He was so sure of himself, so smug. It annoyed her. "I've *never* been in love," she retorted and was satisfied by the startled widening of his eyes.

"How come?"

"Because I've never met anyone who's made me care enough, that's why."

After a silent moment, he said, "I guess I can't argue. You know your own mind, and you've certainly made it clear I'll never be in the running as a candidate."

Somehow she had expected him to give her more of an argument. She was relieved he hadn't, yet at the same time she felt vaguely disappointed. She noticed how the lamplight had softened the arrogant lines of his features without detracting from their masculinity. She also noticed that he must have shaved before coming to the cottage that afternoon, for the lean planes running from his cheekbone to jaw were without stubble.

He had also been examining her, and now his hand moved to idly fluff her hair. "I like all these pretty little curls."

Her nose wrinkled, yet she couldn't suppress a smile at the flattery. "I hate them. It's this damp weather."

"I like them," he insisted. "Everything about your appearance is bandbox perfect except for these unruly red-gold corkscrews. A fascinating contradiction, like this adorable mouth." His fingers left her hair to slip down and outline the subject of discussion. "The words coming from it are proper, even prim, but the mouth itself is so lusciously inviting..."

He kissed the tender corner of her smile, then with a finger, gently parted her lips. She caught her breath as he traced his tongue tip along the sensitive inner flesh, then kissed the other corner.

"Positively wanton," he whispered, then retraced the delicate softness. She felt warmth begin to curl within her as his tender explorations continued, going round and round, never centering, never becoming the kiss her trembling lips were beginning to yearn for. With unconscious intent to increase the pressure of his mouth upon hers she tried to move toward him, but his hand, fingers gentle but firm on either side of her jaw, frustrated her attempt as his teasing ministrations went on and on.

"So sweet," he whispered, "so very sweet," and with his hand still so lightly, but firmly restraining her, he kissed her closed eyelids, her cheeks, and then leisurely resumed that maddening mischief with her mouth.

"Marc..." she uttered breathlessly and at long last he allowed his mouth to center warmly upon hers. As if she were the one who had won a victory, she responded to his kiss with fervor, eagerly seeking to satisfy the hungry need he had so skillfully aroused.

His hand slipped down to her lower back. She welcomed the pressure as their embrace became more impassioned and then she became acutely aware of the male contours against her pliant softness.

"Marc..." she cautioned. "Marc... I think that's enough."

He allowed her to pull free, moving his legs so she could find a place to sit, but then, looking up at her, eyes heavy-lidded, he tried to pull her back down to him.

She shrugged away. "Marc. We'd better leave."

"You're right," he said with a slow, indolent smile, agreeing too readily it seemed, but then he added, "We'll find the bedroom far more comfortable."

His audacity made her catch her breath. She thought for a moment of the chamber she had glimpsed earlier that day: a room with pale gold metallic wallpaper and black lacquer furniture in an Oriental style. Across an expanse of gold carpet, the wide bed had been dressed in a turquoise, white and navy quilted coverlet with draperies that matched. Into her startled mind leaped an erotic vision of herself and Marc in that room, then, shaking her head, she had to laugh.

"You're everything I ever thought! You said you owed Felix favors. Is it because he allows you to use this cottage as a bachelor's lair?"

His smoldering gray eyes danced. "Mmm," he growled. "A lair." Shifting, he propped a pillow behind his shoulders so he sat up higher. "Where do you find your terminology? Yes, a lair. A den of iniquity."

He walked tanned fingers up her arm to her shoulder, but when he again attempted to draw her toward him, she protested, "Marc, I really mean it." Pulling free, she climbed off the couch, rather surprised when he let her go so easily.

"We can't leave these glasses like this," she said, and to her chagrin, heard an unsteadiness in her voice. She walked to the dining room, finding that her legs weren't all that steady either. She took up the glass she had used, then remembered Marc's, which was on the lamp table at the far end of the couch.

She was about to get it, then became acutely aware that he studied her every move with that hot and heavy-lidded stare. An essential maleness seeming to emanate from him as he lounged against the colorful cushions.

Checking her forward motion she steadied herself, ordering crisply, "Bring your glass along so we can clean up."

In the kitchen, she was running water when he came bearing the tiny tulip-shaped goblet that he placed next to hers on the drainboard. Even now, in the brightly lit kitchen, something about his presence struck her as almost overwhelmingly male.

"You're not going to get hot water," he said, his voice a deep rumble.

Caught off guard by so prosaic a statement, she tested the water as if not believing him.

He continued, "Felix always turns off the water heater when he's away for any length of time. If you need it hot, you could put some on the stove to boil. If it's worth it for two glasses, that is."

She thought of the two of them standing awkwardly in the kitchen with nothing to do except wait for water to boil.

"This detergent seems to suds up fine in cold water," she decided. Washing the glasses under running water, she rinsed them well. The domestic chore calmed her, as did Marc's matter-of-fact manner.

"They'd pass any inspection," he observed, holding the first goblet to the light. Having taken a dishtowel from the counter, he dried the glasses, then returned them to the china cupboard in the dining room.

She swished the last soap bubble from the sink and spread the dishtowel to dry. Stepping from the kitchen, she crossed to the living room and switched off the lamp by the couch. The room settled into a hazy darkness, the only light filtering in through the dining area from the kitchen.

As she started to retrace her steps, Marc closed the door to the china cupboard and turned. Whether by design or accident, the broad-shouldered mass of his silhouette was directly in her path. As she tried to step past him, he touched her arm.

"Peri..." His tone held an intense quality that captured her attention. "I just wanted you to know that..." Words seemed to elude him, and then, "Peri, we talked of caring and I want you to know you're a person I could care for...really care..."

She didn't believe him for an instant. Yet, all the same, there was something in his manner that stripped away her defenses, leaving her so desperately *wanting* to believe him that when his arms suddenly enfolded her, she could summon no protest.

As their lips met it was as if everything between them earlier had been only a preliminary for this moment. Longing swept through Peri like a fever.

Lost in a sweet rush of sensations it seemed to her that it no longer made a difference whether or not there could ever be anything permanent between them. She had looked in vain for the right man—a man who might not even exist. So why not have whatever she could find with Marc? From the first, he had attracted and excited her in a way she hadn't dreamed was possible. Refuse him, and there might never be another person able to strike such vital fire within her, a fire that even now swept away the last of her resistance.

Yes, she thought, her breath coming in shallow gasps, *yes.* And she clung to him, willingly, her only desire to be closer to him.

"Peri," he groaned. Sensing her surrender he lifted her into his arms.

The bedroom was lit only dimly by moonlight showing through the draperies. He swept aside the quilted coverlet and settled her upon silken sheets. Hovering over her, he whispered endearments as he kissed and caressed, taking pleasure in her every trembling response as though she were his to savor with all the time in the world.

"So sweet, so precious," came his husky whisper as his hands worked their magic in the darkness. "So soft, so beautiful. I want to see you..." But when he reached toward the bed lamp, she felt stricken by a spasm of shyness.

"No, please don't," she begged, drawing her arms around him, his muscular shoulders smooth under her fingertips. Protected by darkness she pulled him close, making him forget all else.

The warm male scent of him filled her nostrils like a heady wine, her senses reeling as his hands and lips made her sigh and murmur with pleasure, her flesh responding in ways she knew only by instinct. In a glorious daze of sensation, she willed his virile force to conquer her with a storm of passion that would override her lack of experience, but then, as his caresses became more bold, inhibition made her restrain him.

"Peri..." he groaned, perhaps thinking she played some coy game. "I can't get enough of you." Again she gasped and flinched away.

There was a long, frozen silence in which he added things up, then he spoke at last.

"Peri?" His tone was strained. "Peri, when you said you had never been in love, you didn't mean you've never made love—did you?"

The silence that fell between them seemed to last an eternity.

"Peri." His voice took on an ugly rawness. "That is what you meant, isn't it?" He moved back sharply, as if burned. "Lord! It is, isn't it? That's *exactly* what you meant!"

She felt as if she had been slapped.

"Marc...you don't understand."

"Understand?" he derided. "I understand all too well."

"But, Marc..." In misery, she reached toward him, but he shoved her hand aside and jumped up, the mattress jolting. It was as if he couldn't endure the thought of her touch. She heard him fumble for his clothing, then head for the door.

"Marc, please..."

"I'll be waiting for you in the kitchen," he rasped on his way out of the room.

After a stunned moment of disbelief, she switched on the light to find her own clothing. Her fingers seemed to be all thumbs, the buttons not buttoning, the jeans' zipper balking, the slim leather straps of her sandals twisting rebelliously. She kept feeling as if she wanted to cry, but there were no tears. Her mind was blank.

When she smoothed the coverlet back into place she found one of Marc's socks. She picked it up automatically. On her way from the room, a glance into the mirror showed her that her face was unnaturally white and her expression was frozen. She ran a haphazard hand through her curls and inadvertently flicked off an earring. Her ears were pierced, and although she quickly found the pearl-studded gold post, the back was lost somewhere in the plush nap of the rug. Abandoning the search, she mindlessly tucked the piece of jewelry into Marc's sock, then remembering the light, she turned back to switch it off.

Robotlike, she went through the house. When she came to the kitchen, she found Marc standing impatiently at the door leading to the garden. Expression as stoic as hers, he opened it, giving her a wide berth to proceed him. Then he spied his sock.

"I wondered where that was," he muttered, snatching it from her. He switched off the kitchen light and then closed and locked the door. She kept on walking, going out through the garden and heading toward the jeep that stood out clearly in the moonlight. Suddenly, she heard Marc give an astonished howl of pain.

Alarmed, she whirled. He was hopping about, frantically tearing off the sock he had just slipped on.

Remembering, she rushed back to the garden.

"A scorpion!" he cursed as she approached. "A damned scorpion must have crawled into my sock!"

Foot bared, he sank to the patio stones, trying to inspect his injury by the moonlight.

When she reached toward the discarded sock, he yelled angrily. "Didn't you hear what I said? There's something in there!"

"Oh, yes, I know," she said contritely. "The post to my earring." Reaching inside, she withdrew the bright metal.

In a rage, he cursed again. "That damned thing stabbed straight through my foot!"

The way he hollered killed her sympathy. "Here's your sock." Coldly, she dropped it before him and returned to the jeep. She was already inside by the time he arrived, walking with a limp she was sure was exaggerated.

He started the engine, but when he tried to throw the jeep into gear, it stalled. She had a twinge of guilt, thinking his foot might really be hurt after all and giving him trouble with the clutch. She said nothing however, and maintained her silence all the way back to the villa, her hands tightly clasped in her lap. When he pulled in the drive and brought the vehicle to a stop by the light of the front portico, she finally apologized.

"I'm sorry about your foot."

"It's all right," he snapped, starting to climb out.

"And, Marc . . ."

He stopped and glared with narrowed eyes, as if daring her to continue. The light from the portico shadowed his face strangely, making the lines harsh and uncompromising. Her throat felt almost too dry to speak, but she forced herself on.

"Marc, about the other . . . I mean, when we were back at the cottage . . ." To her horror, she started to cry.

"Now what?" he demanded, suddenly furious.

His tone dried her tears instantly. "Nothing." She set her chin. "If you have to be told, then there's nothing to say."

Her sudden calm enraged him even further. He leaned toward her, manner menacing. "You're right there's nothing to say. You've made your low opinion of me clear enough all along, only I happened to be convenient when your mood was right. Do you think I'll risk having you blame me for the rest of your life for some crazy impulse?'' Nostrils flaring, his voice dropped to a low and dangerous growl. "You want somebody just to experiment with, little girl, you can damned well go find somebody else!''

Chapter Eight

Peri's night was a torment of confused emotions.

Thinking things over, it was shamefully clear that she had willingly encouraged Marc to seduce her. She told herself she should be glad nothing had come of it, yet when she remembered the touch of his lips and the thrill of his ardor, forbidden longing sang through her veins. She couldn't deny he had made her want him desperately. So why then, at almost the moment of his triumph, had he backed off?

If he was the man she had believed, her inexperience would never have chilled him. But chilled him it had. She cringed in memory of his icy fury when they returned to the villa. Fortunately, after he strode off, she had managed to creep inside and upstairs without being confronted by Karen, who would have surely bombarded her with questions she was in no mood to answer.

Tossing fitfully, Peri smoothed the silken folds of her nightgown then fluffed her pillow in the vain attempt to find a position in which she could relax. Maybe the tragic loss of Marc's wife had indeed made him fear commitment. If he sought only uncomplicated pleasure in his affairs, no wonder her naiveté had jolted him. What had appeared as a simple erotic game had suddenly taken on potentially serious aspects. She remembered how vehemently he had said he wouldn't risk having her blame him in the future.

Uttering a deep sigh, she had to admit he had shown a restraint she never would have expected. She closed her eyes, willing herself to sleep, yet all she could think of was the rising tide of passion she had experienced in Marc's arms. She sighed again. No matter how she looked at it, he was not quite the careless rogue she had assumed.

In the morning, Peri slipped downstairs before Karen could invade her room. Calling a hello to Margarit, who was setting place mats on the glass-topped breakfast table, she wandered through the latticed Moorish arch that led to the pool. There she found that the morning breeze had scattered jacaranda blossoms over the water's surface. Thoughts still troubled, she watched the bright petals swirl in mysterious patterns, like scarlet tea leaves that could reveal her fortune if only she could read them.

Theo emerged from the house to take his first cup of morning coffee from the silver service waiting on the terrace table. He was soon followed by the others. Peri joined them, not wanting to call attention to herself by making a late entrance.

Marc's greeting was tight-lipped, but not enough so that anyone, except perhaps Karen, noticed anything amiss. Josepha, filled with excited talk about the expedition at El Tajin, dominated the breakfast conversation.

The journey itself would take only a few hours, but the primitive conditions under which the group would live during their week's stay had made a lot of planning necessary. To Peri, it sounded like nothing less than a camping trip. Josepha was busily outlining certain last-minute details when Concepcion appeared with the news of a telephone call.

"Peri, it's my sister wanting to speak with you," Josepha informed after listening to the housekeeper's rapid Spanish.

Estelle was home in the United States after returning from Paris, and as her first words crackled over the line, Peri felt catapulted back to that meeting when the businesswoman's shrewd, all-knowing manner had briskly taken charge of her life.

But then, with a lot less formality than Peri was prepared for, Estelle announced warmly, "From my grandson's report, I have every reason to be delighted with your progress with Karen. Most of all, I'm pleased that she remains in such good spirits. As I had hoped, getting the book under control has helped her. When will it be completed?"

Peri explained about the last few photos that Karen considered necessary and predicted when the entire package would be ready for the publisher.

Estelle responded with enthusiasm. Her manner struck Peri as being uncharacteristically friendly for a conversation with a mere employee. When her comments turned into family chit-chat, Peri was frankly confused. Estelle spoke about Josepha and Theo, then mentioned that she had given Marc another two weeks of vacation.

"He deserves the time off," the woman said with a deprecating laugh. "He could all too easily become a workaholic like his grandmother."

Returning to the breakfast table, Peri was still pondering over Estelle's warmth when she heard Josepha say to Marc, "With you along on the trip, we won't have to pack our gear so tight—not when you can drive the other truck. That also means—"

"If you will allow me to squeeze a word in edgewise," Marc interrupted with a wry smile, "my plans have changed." Deep lines bracketed his mouth, and his eyes, like pale gray frost that morning, made an especially marked contrast to his tan. Looking at him, Peri suddenly realized that he also might have spent a restless night.

"I'm afraid I'll have to fly back to the States instead of going with you tomorrow," he told his aunt, pouring himself more coffee as he spoke. "You know what a slave driver your sister is. After our Paris conference, there are too many things she's depending on me to do."

"Oh, but no," Peri barged in, not thinking. "Estelle just told me most emphatically that she wants you to have two weeks more of vacation, so—"

Marc turned to give Peri the most poisonous look imaginable. "How convenient that you should bring such welcome news, Miss Brendan." Smile as thin as a blade, he set down his cup and folded his arms on the table before him. "Here I was, so certain I would have to forgo the trip and the extended pleasures of your company."

Peri's cheeks flamed, but Josepha, not noticing Marc's sarcasm, whooped and clapped him on the shoulders. "More vacation time? That sister of mine *is* mellowing."

Abashed, Peri looked down at her plate. Obviously, Marc had wanted to change his plans expressly to avoid her. Now, because of her big mouth, they would be thrown together after all. She decided she didn't need devices to tell her fortune: the next few days were guaranteed to be a disaster.

The group left early the next morning. Josepha and Theo were followed by Karen and Peri in the jeep. Last in line was Marc, at the wheel of the truck that carried their heavier supplies. Marc was accompanied by Luis who was planning to spend most of his time there with his parents.

As they jostled along, Peri was all too aware of Marc riding behind them. It seemed she could feel his eyes upon her, critical and sardonic. Since breakfast the previous day he had continued addressing her with such elaborate courtesy that even Josepha began giving him puzzled glances. Just thinking about his behavior made Peri's stomach tighten in a nervous knot. When Karen, who had been chattering away merrily, made a mean remark about Harris, Peri's frayed nerves snapped.

"Karen, how can you be so rotten?" she accused, adjusting her sunglasses as she glared at the girl. "Harris is an old friend of mine and a thoroughly nice person. This morning, you could have at least managed to say goodbye to him."

Karen's round face looked blank. "But I did!"

With a scornful sniff, Peri recalled the woebegone expression on Harris's bearded face as he stood forgotten on the sidelines, hopelessly watching Karen pay attention to everyone but him. "Sure, you gave him an offhand wave that just as easily could have been for Concepcion or any of the other servants. You know he came from the work area especially to see you off. You could have at least spared a few personal words."

"And what would that have accomplished?" Karen returned, tossing her head smartly. "It would only be giving him false encouragement. Isn't that even more cruel?''

Peri narrowed her eyes. "Every time somebody tries to talk to you about Harris, you go into a who-cares act. But underneath the joking, it's a different story, isn't it?''

"I don't know what you mean.''

Peri took another tack. "Harris thinks you still care about him.''

Karen hooted. "Look who's joking now!''

"I think he's right. At least, I think you have a lot more feeling for him than you're willing to admit.''

"Well, you're wrong.''

Peri remained stubborn. "I don't think so.''

An intense rush of emotion wiped all playfulness from Karen's expression. "A lot you know, Peri Brendan!'' she cried in agitation, glaring at her companion. "Have I been pestering you about what happened between you and Marc yesterday? No. So by what right are you nagging me about Harris?'' Her voice was shrill. "I thought you came to Veracruz to help me out and to be my friend. Instead all you've done is ruin everything!''

A bump caused the jeep to swerve and Karen whipped her attention back to her driving, but not before Peri had seen tears spring into the girl's eyes.

Peri was so taken aback by Karen's accusations that she could only stare in speechless surprise. Mentally, she replayed the conversation, but could find no clue to explain why Karen had suddenly become so distraught. It almost sounded as if the girl blamed her for some sort of betrayal.

Upset, she turned her attention to her surroundings. Their route had wound inland, the countryside losing the tropical lushness of the coast. Peri could look in any direction and see nothing but a monotony of low, green hills, many planted with corn. Even though it was still morning, the sun was a brassy glare, making her eyes sting despite her dark glasses.

After many miserable miles of riding in silence, Peri saw Theo and Josepha turn onto a narrow lane. Up ahead, the hills were interspersed with huge mounds of fire-blackened rubble. From what Karen had told her previously, Peri understood that these mounds were the ruins of what had once been the temples of a sacred city. Burning off centuries of overgrown vegetation was the first step in gaining access to the building stones so that the structures could be rebuilt.

Karen jounced the jeep over a rough, steep lane, then rounded a hill, coming onto a flat area of scrub grass. Vehicles were parked near a long shed with a roof thatched with banana leaves. A cluster of people stood talking to a man garbed in the white blouse and white trousers of the native Totonoc Indians.

"The others are already here," Karen said, seeing the colleagues of her aunt and uncle.

"Oh, that's good!" Peri crowed with exaggerated animation, thinking it would be a mistake not to acknowledge the first words Karen had seen fit to speak in nearly an hour.

They climbed from the jeep, Peri aware that Marc, who had brought the truck to a stop behind them, was also getting out. Catching her gaze, he mockingly doffed an imaginary hat and bowed. Flushing, Peri turned with a sinking feeling to follow Karen who was already walking toward her aunt and uncle. Marc obviously had no intention of forgiving her for buttonholing him into the trip, and if Karen didn't recover from her bad mood, the next few days were going to be even more of an ordeal than she had feared.

Josepha and Theo introduced them to Esteban, the Indian who would be their cook during their stay, then to their colleagues—three men and a woman, all in their mid-sixties. Peri learned they were part of the group who had approved the grant for Karen's book of photographs. All were garbed in well-worn khaki's and they seemed pleasant, but vague about anything that didn't have to do with their cherished interest in anthropology.

"Museum types," Peri joked in an aside to Karen, hoping to make her laugh, using a term the girl had applied when speaking of them previously. Karen, determined to coddle her foul mood, offered no response.

Under Theo's direction, the members of the group learned where they were to erect their tents. The anthropologists went about the task efficiently, making it clear they had set up camp thousands of times. When Luis brought over the tent that Karen and Peri were to use, Peri was determined to do the same. After all, she had once been in the Girl Scouts, hadn't she?

As the two women started work, Marc, aided by Luis, finished removing supplies from the truck. Impelled by the noonday rise of the sun, he had shucked off his shirt. The sheen of sweat on his lean, muscular torso played up a masculine perfection that kept drawing Peri's eyes against her will. She also had to secretly admit she was favorably impressed by Marc's manner with Luis. From overheard snatches of conversation, she appreciated his knack for mingling instruction and praise in such a way that the work was enjoyable for them both.

When the truck was unloaded, Marc sent the youth off to help Josepha and the others, then set up his own tent by himself.

Peri began to realize that she and Karen were running into trouble around the time Marc finished. Rubbing her back, which felt broken, she stared balefully at the green canvas that lay sprawled on the ground like a deflated balloon. Her arms ached from hauling on the stiff, heavy mass, and her blouse was soaked with perspiration. From the corner of her eye, she saw Marc looking in their direction. The fact that they were stuck was obvious, only instead of coming over to see what he could do, he turned his attention to organizing the piles of supplies taken from the truck. Peri decided she would rather be shot than request his help.

Irritably, she turned to Karen, who was childishly showing she was still angry by being as uncooperative as possible. "Come on," Peri snapped. "You know we can't put up the center pole until we fasten down the sides. There has to be tent stakes somewhere. Where are they?"

"They're here somewhere," came the surly reply.

On that scorching day, Karen had illogically worn her hair loose rather than braiding it, and the thick dark strands kept falling around her shoulders in sticky-looking, untidy tangles. Peri scowled in exasperation. On one hand, she wanted to mother the girl—to stroke her hair and ask, "What's the trouble Karen—let's talk it over," while on the other hand, she wanted to slap her for behaving like a five-year-old.

Voice sharp, Peri said, "Well if they are here, then we've somehow got them lost underneath the canvas." She shuddered at the notion of wrestling with the heavy fabric to search for them.

"They're here," repeated Karen, jaw set, as if her insistence alone would magically make them appear.

Fate, having taken pity on them at last, sent Marc striding across the coarse grass of the clearing. Bearing a rope-tied bundle of stakes, he said to his sister, "Sometimes I wonder where your head is at, Karen. Look what I just found."

Studiously ignoring Peri, he handed over the stakes. His hair was plastered to his forehead and rivulets of sweat had matted the black tangle on his bare chest. Attention still focused on Karen, he said, "They were in with a sack of tools where you must have dropped them months ago. Typical of you—just too dratted lazy to put things where they belong. If I hadn't found them by accident, they might never have shown up."

Karen's bad mood expanded generously to include her brother. "What am I supposed to do now? Get on my hands and knees to thank you?" She threw the stakes to the ground. "I didn't put them in the wrong place. They must have fallen out of my tent roll. Somebody else put them with the tools."

His tone was lofty. "Again, typical. Don't forget you lived in my house for almost a year. I'm familiar with all your lame excuses."

"It isn't an excuse!" Karen defended indignantly. "I put my gear away perfectly. And how dare you make it sound as if I caused problems in your house? Julie never complained."

Marc laughed, but the undertone was biting. "Julie never complained about anything as long as she didn't have to be responsible for it. What she let you get away with was criminal."

"You take that back!" Karen shouted, exploding into what could only be called a tantrum. "Take it back, Marc—you take it back!" Like a little wildcat, she flung herself upon him, scratching and screaming, beating her fists on his chest and trying to strike his face.

"What in the devil—" Thunderstruck, he absorbed the fury of her attack for a moment, then pinioned her wrists in his hands. She attempted to struggle out of his grasp, then, finding it impossible, she collapsed in a hysterical fit of weeping.

Marc, his eyes filled with confusion, held his sister as her wild tears continued. He had gone deathly white under his tan.

Not knowing what to do, Peri touched Karen on the shoulder, and with that touch, the girl suddenly turned and fell into Peri's arms.

"It isn't true what he said," she sobbed frantically. "Julie was wonderful! I told you how I felt about her. I loved her Peri, I really loved her! What he said wasn't true."

"That's all right. I know, I know," crooned Peri, rocking Karen in her arms.

When her soothing began to have a quieting effect, Peri looked at Marc over the still-weeping girl's head. "Look, your tent is already up. Is there some place in there where she can lie down?"

He reacted slowly, as if unable to gather his thoughts. "Oh, sure. I'll fix something." He hurried ahead, and by the time Peri helped Karen into the tent, he had a cot ready.

Still speaking in soothing tones, Peri got Karen settled and pulled a sheet over her.

"I'll stay awhile," she whispered to Marc, who nodded and left. For some time the girl's body shook with deep sobs, but the emotional storm had exhausted her and she finally drifted into sleep.

When Peri quietly slipped outside, she found Marc waiting, his shirt back on, his hair combed. She saw he had finished putting up the tent that she and Karen were to use.

Shrugging off her thanks, he asked anxiously, "How's Karen doing?"

"Asleep, for now."

He grunted. "I guess that's for the best." He didn't sound particularly convinced. He glanced over to where Josepha and the other anthropologists sat perched on camp stools, chatting and renewing their friendship after getting their quarters ship-shape. "Preoccupied or not, there was no way that crew could have missed the commotion over here. I went over and did my best to assure them that everything was under control." He sighed. "I only wish I could believe it myself."

Peri noticed that Marc was rather pale—he still looked shaken. She thought they should sit down and motioned toward the shade of the truck.

"Come over here," she suggested, and he followed mechanically, as if temporarily unable to reason for himself. Reaching the shade, she took a seat on one of the supply boxes and he followed suit.

He rubbed a shaking hand over his face. "I should have known to avoid any discussion with Karen that included Julie." His tone was as unsteady as his hand. "The trouble is, she's seemed so much better lately that I just didn't think."

Wondering if she risked getting her head bitten off if she continued the discussion, Peri ventured, "Karen once talked to me about Julie."

Marc, his eyes bleak, showed no surprise. It was as if any antagonism he had felt toward Peri was forgotten. "Karen worshiped her. Julie was my wife, you know. When she died, it hit Karen awfully hard."

"And that happened when Karen was fourteen, right?" Peri was already sure of the answer. She sounded annoyed. "That was the bad experience that was the start of Karen's depression. What was the point of keeping it such a gigantic mystery?''

Marc hesitated, perhaps remembering the day he told Peri the subject was none of her business. Then he lifted his broad shoulders in a weary shrug. ''At the time, it seemed better not to talk about it.'' His scarred eyebrow tilted as he managed a humorless grin. ''Sort of letting sleeping dogs lie. That theory sure backfired.''

''It sure did,'' agreed Peri, seeing the scratch that Karen's fingernails had left on his cheek. She shifted her position, longing in vain for a breath of a breeze. Even in the shade, the heat was punishing. Adjusting the scarf that held her hair up off her neck, she tried to recall Marc's exact words to his sister.

''What set Karen off?'' she asked with a frown. ''The fact that you seemed to be criticizing Julie?''

''I suppose. Because I said Julie let Karen get by with things. Which was true,'' he added defensively.

''Well, she certainly went up like a sky rocket.''

''Yes, but I've never seen her violent before—against someone else, I mean. Usually, she only hurts herself.''

''You mean like breaking off with Harris?''

Not answering, he tilted his head back, closing his eyes wearily. Before the incident with his sister, he had seemed filled with energy despite the heat. Now he looked haggard and depleted. It was as if he had instantly aged. Peri wondered if he had looked that way when he returned from the hospital after his wife died. He must have loved Julie so much, she thought, and was ashamed at the irrational jealousy that jabbed her.

She decided that Marc wasn't going to make any further comment, but then he said, ''Sometimes, when she's in her blue moods, I really become frightened for her. There just seems no reason for her to wound herself as she does. What triggers such despair?'' Opening his eyes, he spread his hands in a helpless gesture. "I love Karen—I want her to be happy, yet I keep seeing her deliberately turn her back on her chances."

He closed his eyes again, speaking in a hoarse whisper. "Peri, there's something very wrong in my sister's life and I don't know how to help."

Instinctively, Peri reached out, laying a comforting hand on his, as if it were the most natural thing in the world to do. He turned his hand so that it grasped hers. His grip was desperate, like a drowning man reaching for help. Something intense seemed to vibrate through the air and Peri trembled. Holding her breath, trying not to move, she strove to do nothing that would disturb the moment. Slowly, Marc's grip relaxed although he still held her hand. She saw the tension on his face begin to ebb, as if he were able to draw strength from the communication of her touch.

Luis chose that moment to burst upon them, asking Marc if it was time to drive him to his parent's home.

Marc opened his eyes, his expression dazed. With reluctance, he released Peri's hand.

"I'm all ready as you can see, Señor Marc," the youth continued, proudly presenting a freshly scrubbed face and spotless hands. His jet-black hair showed streaks from a wet comb, and he wore a T-shirt Marc must have brought from France—one stenciled with a drawing of the Mona Lisa. A balloon emerging from her famed smile read Paris Turns Me On.

With effort, Marc lifted his mood to meet the boy's enthusiasm. Standing, he said heartily, "You look terrific, Luis. We can leave right away. You know, I never thought you'd get those grubby paws clean after all that hard work unloading the truck."

The youth beamed, his large, white teeth flashed brightly.

"That's some shirt!" Peri approved, feeling she should say something.

Luis giggled. "Should I tell her about the other shirt, Señor Marc?"

"Sure." Having got himself under control, the twinkle had returned to Marc's eyes.

Luis tried to speak, but his giggles became uncontrollable.

"I cannot! It is too silly. You say it to the *señorita*, okay? I'll run and tell Señora Josepha we are leaving."

"What kind of disgraceful shirt did you buy for the child?" Peri demanded, glad for the change of mood.

Chuckling, Marc climbed into the driver's seat of the truck and closed the door. Speaking out the open window, he said, "It's similar to the one Luis is wearing now. It shows a grinning gargoyle with a balloon that reads: The Mona Lisa Turns Me On."

Luis, panting, raced back and climbed into the passenger seat. "Did he tell you?" he asked, looking across Marc at Peri. Her laugh gave him his answer. "It is silly, no? But I like it." Playfully, he poked at Marc's shoulder. "This hombre here, he knows good shirts."

"You tell her, kid!" applauded Marc, then sobering, he turned back to Peri. His eyes were again shrouded with worry. "Luis's family will probably want me to stay and have supper at the village but I suppose I shouldn't. Karen will—"

"Don't worry about her," Peri assured. It seemed she could still feel his hand gripping hers. "Don't worry," she repeated. "She'll be okay. I'll keep a close watch."

Chapter Nine

After Marc left, Theo, jauntily sporting an explorer's hat, came over to ask Peri if she and Karen would like to join their group for a short walk to the ruins of the sacred city.

Peri smiled at the older man, shaking her head. She was curious about El Tajin, but that could wait. "Thanks, but Karen is still sleeping. I'll stay here with her."

Theo nodded, the bright sunlight glinting on his glasses. "How is she?" The worry in his tone belied the calm of his manner.

Peri wasn't sure how much to explain. "Marc said something and Karen became upset. He didn't understand her reaction any better than I did."

Sighing, Theo slipped off his hat and rubbed a hand over his bald head. "Our Karen can be hard to figure out. One time or another, we've all discovered that." He patted Peri's shoulder. "Thank you for watching over her.

In this heat, we probably won't be gone long and we won't be far away." He stuck out an arm, pointing. "If you need us, we can be back in a jiffy. Just go around the next hill or two and holler."

After the group left, Peri, feeling exhausted, decided to take a nap. She carried her sleeping bag into Marc's tent and settled near Karen. The canvas enclosure had a distinctive smell, a kind of crisp, heated oiliness that she remembered from girlhood camp-outs. She stared up at the fabric slant of the roof, seeing that its green expanse was pricked with imperfections that made it glimmer with tiny, brilliant dots as the sunlight struck through.

Tired as she was, she did not sleep right away. Her thoughts kept returning to that moment when Marc had clasped her hand so desperately in his.

She began to recognize that her feelings about him had undergone a complete change. Since that evening at the cottage, she had begun thinking of him in a new way. She felt a queer sensation when she realized that Karen's prediction was right: she'd fallen in love with him. How ironic then that the very situation that had made her start to see him differently had also thoroughly discouraged his interest. Or had it? She thought again of his actions that afternoon. At that moment, he had needed her. Whether he knew it or not, he had needed her.

Finally she fell into a restless doze, and about an hour later, when she heard the others return, she got up. The air in the enclosure was stifling despite a mesh-covered window opening. Returning to her own tent, she changed from her wrinkled blouse into a fresh one, a yellow chambray with short sleeves. Outside, Josepha called her to come join the others for an iced drink. Sitting with them under the long shelter, Peri was grateful to find the welcome miracle of a breeze. Relaxing, she gave herself a manicure while listening to the group discuss their plans for exploring El Tajin the following day.

Karen didn't stir for the rest of the afternoon, and at suppertime, when she was shaken awake, she resisted, wanting only to retreat back into sleep.

"I'm fine. I don't need anything," she whined fretfully, pushing heavy, dark strands of hair from her face. "Just leave me alone."

"Come on, you have to eat," Peri cajoled, but Karen wouldn't move. Peri finally brought her a tray of the spicy meat and rice mixture that Esteban had prepared and then diplomatically left, figuring that the girl would be too stubborn to eat if she remained present.

When Peri returned to the group, she was headed off by Josepha for a private talk. Like her companions, the woman wore khaki-colored pants and shirt, but a bold red, black and yellow scarf at the throat made the outfit uniquely her own.

"Theo tells me Karen was all stirred up over something Marc said," Josepha began without preliminary. Sincere concern showed through her brash manner, and Peri decided this was the time to confide in her.

"Yes. He made a critical remark about Julie that offended Karen. She really flew into him."

Josepha uttered a sound of dismay. "Marc should have known better. Karen thought the sun rose and set on Julie." The way Josepha tilted her head emphasized the slant of her eyes. "You did know about Marc's marriage, didn't you? I mean, you knew he was married to Julie?"

"I know her name, but that's about all." Peri hoped her words would encourage Josepha to reveal more, and they did.

"Well, Julie came along just when Marc was thinking he should settle down. Talk about perfect timing! That romance took off like wildfire and they were married almost before we knew it. She was a darling thing, an only child whose mother had died when she was born. Her father treated her like a princess, and she even looked the part—like a little painted doll that would shatter if you as much as sneezed in her direction. She should have been spoiled rotten, only, by some miracle she wasn't. But she did have a sugar-sweet view of life, as if everything automatically had to go her way."

"Karen said she was very beautiful," Peri interjected, again aware of that painful stab of jealousy.

"She made the ideal bride. Everyone said she and Marc were a storybook couple—she, so tiny and fair, he, so tall and handsome. Sadly, there wasn't much time for the happily-ever-after part because while they were on their honeymoon, Julie's father keeled over dead with a heart attack. Marc rushed Julie home, but she was so distraught she couldn't even attend the funeral. I think she would have gone out of her mind if she hadn't had Marc to cling to."

"It must have been awfully hard for her," sympathized Peri, remembering how adrift she had felt when first stricken by her own father's death.

"You said a mouthful there. Life can't always be roses, but that's what Julie was apparently brought up to expect. It's no wonder she fell apart when her dad died. All things considered, I suppose she acted as brave as she could manage." Josepha smiled, shrugging off the bad memories. "And of course, once she was over her grief, things were fine."

"When did Karen go live with them?"

"Oh, let's see." Josepha tugged at her scarf, as if the gesture would somehow jog her memory. "Theo and I were off on an expedition, and when we returned, Karen was at their house. I guess they had been married for something like two years. We spent part of the holiday with them. Marc was clearly the center of Julie's existence." The woman's smile became bawdy. "As far as I could see, their life together had become one long honeymoon."

Again that stab. "Karen did say they were unusually devoted."

"They were, so I was surprised when they agreed to have Karen move in with them. I was also surprised when that bossy sister of mine allowed it. But she knew Karen wasn't happy living with her, and the move worked out great. As I've said, Karen worshiped Julie. With Julie and Marc being so much older, it must have been as if she had got her parents back again." Josepha's smile faded. "But then, of course, that's also why it was such a blow when Julie died."

Peri winced, thinking how awful it must have been for Marc as well. "I guess the unexpectedness made it especially difficult. Karen said no one even knew Julie was pregnant."

"True," confirmed Josepha, "but afterward, I could look back and see that Julie hadn't been acting her usual self. She always was a jumpy little thing, but she seemed even more nervous during those last few weeks." She shook her head. "I've often wondered if she didn't suspect her pregnancy, but held off going to the doctor. In many ways she was an awfully private person. If she had gone, the doctor might have discovered whatever was wrong in time to save her life. That's one of those things we'll never know," she added with a sigh as she and Peri moved to rejoin the others around a small campfire that had just been lit.

In between checking on Karen, who, after eating only a little had retreated into a deep sleep, Peri spent the rest of the evening being entertained by the anthropologist's scholarly, but exotic tales of adventure. As the sun went down, the air became somewhat cooler, yet was still humid, the sluggish breeze bringing primitive murmurs from hidden insects and the occasional shrill cry of a night bird. The tiny fire, so unnecessary for heat, nevertheless provided a comfortable rallying point as darkness closed round about.

Marc failed to return. Theo was of the opinion that he had elected to stay overnight in the village with Luis and his parents.

At eleven, the group decided to say good-night. Josepha told Peri she didn't see any point in disturbing Karen. "Since Marc is apparently staying out, leave her in his tent and you sleep there, too."

"Okay, but I'll have to get my cot."

"I'll get it," offered Theo, and a few minutes later it was set up next to Karen in Marc's tent. Even though Theo had been unable to help making some noise, Karen had never once stirred from her drug-like depths.

"Anything else you need from your tent?" Theo asked.

"Just my suitcase and I can get that myself, thanks."

Theo doused the last of the campfire and had just disappeared into the enclosure he shared with Josepha when Marc drove in. Surprised by his unexpected return, Peri watched with mixed emotions. She realized that while she was learning more and more about him, she still didn't know how to fit it all together—especially where she was concerned. After what she had heard that afternoon about Julie, she realized she probably would never stand a chance with him.

The starlight cast a strange, misty glow over the scene, making it look like an old black-and-white film. Marc carefully parked the jeep and kept the sound of the engine quiet so as to disturb no one in the darkened scattering of canvas enclosures. When he got out, his tall, broad-shouldered figure appeared almost phantomlike in the eerie light, the flaps of his open shirt casting deep shadows on his bare chest. He crossed the green that divided the camping grounds from the parking area, not seeing Peri until he was almost upon her.

He stopped, surprised. "I figured everyone had turned in."

"I guess I'm the last holdout." Her voice was hushed in the sultry darkness. "And it's a good thing I stayed up, or you'd be in for a shock. The management has switched our rooms."

He cocked his head. "Run that one by me again?"

His voice was steady, as was his stance, but Peri realized he had been drinking. Perhaps just enough to muddle his thoughts.

She explained, "We didn't expect you back tonight. Karen's still in your tent, so I'm spending the night there, too."

"How's she doing?"

Peri sighed. "I'm hoping she'll sleep off her bad mood and wake up fine tomorrow."

"We can always hope." He didn't sound particularly optimistic. "Round-the-clock sleeping is what she's done in the past when heading for a tailspin." He wearily passed a hand over his face. "If this is going to be another one of her bad times, I—"

His voice broke with emotion and it seemed to embarrass him. "God," he muttered. "If I ever load up on tequila again after the kind of day I've had, I should be shot."

Peri noticed that the odor of alcohol wasn't really that strong. She wondered if he wasn't more affected by exhaustion and concern over his sister than by whatever amount he had drunk.

He rubbed his face again. "Is all our stuff switched around too?"

"My suitcase is still over in my tent. I don't know where your things are. Probably still here."

"Okay. Wait while I get my duffel bag, then I'll walk over and help you get your things."

When he rejoined her, bag hefted over his shoulder, she asked about Luis. "Did you get him settled in all right?"

He chuckled, sounding more alert. "Yes. His father has finally landed a good job, and things are going better for the family. There was a tequila party to celebrate the boy's homecoming. That's why I got back so late."

"Homecoming? You mean he won't be returning to the villa?"

"Oh, sure, this is just a visit. With seven brothers and sisters he's always been lost in the shuffle. He really flourishes under the special attention he gets from Concepcion."

Reaching her tent, Peri slipped inside, Marc just behind her. He set down his bag. The flap dropped down behind him, leaving the enclosure pitch black.

"I've got a flashlight right here." Peri congratulated herself for the foresight of leaving a light where she could easily find it after dark. Kneeling, she reached confidently toward the corner where she had left it, but found nothing.

"Theo must have shifted things around when he fetched my cot," she said, still groping. Moving toward her, Marc muttered something about having a portable lamp in his duffel bag. She was going to simply ask him to hold the tent flap open when her searching hand encountered her suitcase.

"I found my luggage, so I don't need a light, thanks," she told him over her shoulder, starting to get up.

"Okay, but I'll—"

Whatever he had been about to say was forgotten as he uttered a startled exclamation. Without warning, he lurched against her, knocking her off balance. She tripped over her suitcase and sprawled to the floor. He landed heavily beside her. There was a stunned moment for both of them, then, voice near her ear, he said dryly, "I found your flashlight—with my foot."

Recovering, she teased, "Sure. What an excuse for stumbling about. That must have been some party! I'd hate to see the kind of shirt Luis would get you to commemorate the occasion."

"The least you could do is thank me for locating your light."

"Thank you." In the darkness, she could not see him at all. "You're not hurt, are you?"

"Only my pride."

They both started to get up at the same time and his shoulder thunked against her head.

She laughed. "This is too much. Maybe we can rent ourselves out for bit parts in a Three Stooges film."

Laughter was both a release and a relief. After the miserable day and all her concerns for Karen, it felt wonderful to find something silly and funny to joke about. And, considering the strain that had been between them, it was especially wonderful to be sharing the moment with Marc.

Apparently feeling much the same way, he joined her laughter. "Hey, how about an Abbot and Costello remake? Instead of being bit players, we could be the stars."

"Right. I'll play Abbot with my clothes stuffed with pillows. You could knock me into next week and I'd never risk a bruise." She frowned. "Abbot *was* the chubby one, wasn't he?"

"No, the chubby one was Costello. But there isn't a director in the world who would allow you to bury that gorgeous figure in a pile of pillows."

She smiled in the darkness at his flattery. "Hollywood, here we come!"

Chuckling, he reached out in the darkness, finding her arm. "Now, let's see if we can master the routine of getting to our feet without further concussions."

As he started to help her up she was suddenly so aware of his physical presence that her smile faded, her breath catching in her throat. His masculine nearness and the warmth of his hand conspired in a heady rush of emotions that made her almost dizzy.

"Marc..." she began, having no idea of anything she wanted to say, simply delighting in the pleasure of whispering his name. His hand tightened on her arm.

She felt his breath on her cheek and moved so it mingled with her own, the open invitation of her manner achingly apparent.

Their lips met, their kiss whirling them both away with its urgent intensity. Peri's thoughts scattered in a thousand directions. Nothing seemed to exist except the rapturous sensations spreading through her veins as Marc's strong arms closed around her.

Sinking back to the floor, she responded to his embrace with an eagerness that would have shocked her had she troubled to reason it out. She stroked along his shoulders and down his back, thrilling to the warm, hard muscles rippling under her touch as he molded his virile frame against her softness.

"Peri..." Whispering endearments, his voice was low and husky with the intensity of powerful emotions brought almost too quickly to the flash point.

Glorying in the moment, her body felt liquid, almost molten, her senses delirious with yearnings. As she lifted her arms to hold him closer, her blouse slipped free at the waist. She heard him draw his breath sharply as he encountered the warm seduction of satin flesh, then with a groan of unleashed response, he sent his hands upward under her blouse, the buttons tearing free as he reached to enfold the sweet fullness of her breasts. Startled, she gasped.

"Peri...?" He spoke with sudden hesitation, her outcry making him aware of the almost violent edge to his desire.

"No. Marc...please." Her pleading command was intended to reassure him, but he, misunderstanding, drew back.

"I'm sorry." His tone was stunned. "I don't know what I was thinking. I just went out of my head. It must have been all that tequila."

Swept with sick dismay, she realized he was attributing his ardent responses to nothing but drunken lust.

"No, Marc," she whispered, knowing that right or wrong, she had welcomed his lovemaking. "Marc, I wanted—"

He cut her off. "God, I'm sorry, Peri. I think...I guess I tore your blouse."

"You didn't. It was just the buttons." Her voice was choked. "Marc, I—"

"Still, it was unforgivable," he interrupted in shame. "Did I hurt you?" And then, he repeated, "I just lost my head."

Hearing him once again attribute his passion to nothing more than a loss of control, she was suddenly furious.

"You didn't hurt me," she snapped. "And stop apologizing. You didn't do a single thing I didn't want you to do—except stop, that is."

The silence from him was so complete that Peri found herself straining her eyes in the darkness, wishing she had some clue as to his expression.

"You wanted me to go on?" he asked at last, sounding as if he sincerely sought an answer, yet she was certain she also heard a thread of scorn weaving through the deep timbre of his voice. With a sinking sensation, she decided that not seeing his expression was a good thing. God forgive me, she thought, but with a sop like Julie for his true beloved, she should have known his opinion of assertive females.

Feeling it no longer mattered what she said, she heedlessly retorted, "If you can suddenly want somebody just because she's within reach, why should it be different for me? I once told you I was human enough, remember? Maybe we both lost our heads."

His chuckle was unexpected. "Maybe so, but I don't remember you trying to rip off my clothes."

His amusement enraged her further. "So macho! You have to take all the responsibility, don't you? If you feel so bad about a bit of damage to my blouse, suppose you do something worthwhile about it." She grabbed his hand.

"What's this?" he demanded as she pressed a small object into his palm.

"One of the buttons. And here…" She felt around the canvas floor. "Here's another one. That still leaves one missing, but sewing on those two will be good enough."

"Hold on there. You can't expect—"

"I not only can, I do. I'm sure Josepha will have some sort of needle and thread available." And then, having slipped off her blouse in the protective darkness, she thrust that at him as well.

"Now wait just a moment." Hearing him balk, Peri expected him to argue further against the sewing task, but instead, he said something far different. "I won't feel right about this unless I can replace all three buttons."

She was caught off guard for a moment, then answered sharply, "That's no problem. Make a sacrifice from one of your own shirts."

"No, that wouldn't be right. It has to be one that belongs."

"How cute," she scorned, thinking she was on to him. "Suddenly you're a perfectionist who won't do anything unless you can do it all."

"That's unfair." He sounded hurt. "I simply refuse to settle for halfway. We'll just have to relocate the missing button."

Something about his tone made her suspicious, but before she could even begin to think what he might be up to, a light blazed. Recoiling, she dashed her hands to her glare-blinded eyes, belatedly remembering he had her flashlight. An instant later, after a second belated recollection, she snatched her hands from her eyes and covered her bare breasts.

"What a rotten trick!" she stormed, feeling like a fool. As her eyes adjusted, she saw he was innocently beaming the light on the floor. The pearlized white button leaped into view.

"There—not lost after all!" Grinning devilishly, he triumphantly held the button aloft. It was an unmistakable parody of the way she had earlier displayed the post of her earring.

Then, eyebrow hooking upward, pretending to just become aware of her half-naked state, he asked curiously, "Not that I object, but the starlight outside is fairly bright. Do you intend to walk over to the other tent dressed like that?"

The dilemma had never occurred to her, but she needn't have worried because he was all too happy to supply a solution. Observing the way she held her arms protectively over her chest, his eyes twinkled mischievously. "I guess you'll have to open your suitcase and take out something to wear, won't you? Well, go to it. I'll assist by holding the light."

Seeing how he had cornered her, she gritted her teeth. "You'll assist by turning *off* the light!"

He shrugged and obediently did as she asked, but as soon as he heard her fumble with the suitcase locks, he asked helpfully, "Are you sure you won't need the light?"

"I'm sure." She realized she couldn't trust him. "Hand over my blouse."

"The one I'm supposed to fix?"

"Very funny. Quit putting on a big act and give it to me."

"That hardly seems fair. Since I tore the buttons loose, I really should wait until—"

"Just give it to me!"

"If you insist."

She heard him drop her blouse to the suitcase. Grabbing it, she ordered, "And you keep that light off!"

He didn't reply, which was somehow more nerveracking than any answer she could imagine. Putting her back to him, she slipped into her blouse as quickly as possible. She tied the loose ends snugly at her midriff and got to her feet.

"Will you want help carrying your suitase?" he asked, not stirring from his position on the floor. She could tell from his voice that he was grinning.

Not answering, she started to leave, but because the flap was closed, she couldn't find the opening right away. Now that she needed the light, of course, he wouldn't supply it, and she surely wouldn't ask. Becoming more exasperated by the second, she batted around like a trapped fly until she found her way out.

Still frothing with emotion, she reached the other tent. Inside, Karen's breathing told her that the girl still slept soundly. Thankfully, the netted window let in enough of the hazy starlight to show Peri her cot.

As she felt around in her suitcase for her nightclothes, her mind whirled with thoughts of Marc. Every supple inch of her flesh still seemed to burn deliciously from his touch. She had begun to see the comic side to the business about her blouse, but that did nothing to ease her mind—or body—when she considered their thwarted lovemaking. With despair, she realized there could not remain the slightest doubt in her mind that she was in love with him. Had she unconsciously imagined their union would bind him to her? If so, it had backfired. After her rash words, he undoubtedly saw the incident as a combination of drunken lechery on his part and simply another attempt at sensual experimentation on hers.

And, since nothing had resulted, he saw no reason to take any of it seriously.

Starting to cry, she realized her actions had done nothing except put further distance between them. She might as well have left Veracruz instead of coming on the trip. Karen's work was done except for the last few photos and the girl could have finished the project without further help. Looking back, Peri recalled it was something she said during the morning ride that upset Karen in the first place. Swept with self-blame, she decided that if she had flown on home, it would have been better for everybody.

Tears rolling down her cheeks, she struggled with the knot she had tied in her blouse and only succeeded in breaking a fingernail. She cursed under her breath. Couldn't anything go right? Karen was in a dangerous depression and she was miserable because she had fallen for a man whose idea of a perfect woman was far different from herself. As for Marc, the cause of half the trouble, he was no doubt laughing himself to sleep, thinking of nothing except how clever he had been to outwit her about the blouse. A blouse that had just caused her to wreck a fresh manicure.

The blouse was the last straw.

Damn it, she thought, her frustrations boiling over. That was one trick she wouldn't let him get away with. Slipping into a knit shirt, she went out into the night, the offending garment in hand. Marc had a light on, probably his portable lamp. She could see his standing figure silhouetted against the canvas.

Not caring whether he had been forewarned by the sounds of her approach or not, she yanked open his tent flap without preliminary. Apparently he had heard nothing, for barefoot, wearing only his jeans, he stared in blind surprise toward the darkened doorway, his body instinctively tensing.

The lamp placed on the floor sculptured the rippling flatness of his stomach, the heavy, muscular armor of his broad chest and the potential power of his arms. Like a warrior, he was on guard against whatever threat might befall, and at the feet of all this magnificent preparedness, Peri reached in and lightly tossed the harmless yellow blouse.

"I do hope you haven't misplaced those buttons," she told him with saccharin sweetness. "And please be quick about it, okay? I'd like to have this back sometime tomorrow."

Chapter Ten

When Peri awoke, light spilling in through the mesh window made a dazzling splotch of gold on the canvas floor. Karen was already up and getting dressed, her freshly washed hair arranged in its customary thick, single braid and tied with a blue ribbon. Peri watched her pull on slacks and a blue, terry-cloth tank top, smoothing it over her rounded hips. She then reached for socks and sturdy leather walking shoes.

It appeared the girl must have recovered her good spirits and Peri felt vastly relieved. Sitting up, she yawned and stretched, determined not to allow herself a single thought of Marc. Stretching again, she called in a companionable way, "Beautiful morning, isn't it?"

"If you think so," Karen muttered uncooperatively, not looking up. Finished with her shoes, she stood and headed for the tent opening.

Disappointed, Peri stared after the disappearing figure. "Well, hip hip hooray, another great day," she sighed under her breath, then tried to cheer herself. Even if Karen was being sullen, she was at least up and moving under her own steam. Maybe breakfast would bring further improvement. Swinging her legs over the edge of her cot, she closed her eyes to the disorder on Karen's side of the enclosure and got herself dressed.

Outside, the air was crystal clear and the breeze was sprightly, promising a day far less oppressive than the previous one.

Within the next twenty minutes people started gathering for breakfast. Marc was among the missing and Josepha ordered Esteban to pour the freshly perked coffee. "The smell will bring those slowpokes galloping back in a jiffy," she predicted heartily, explaining that a group had gotten up early to watch the sunrise from a restored temple known as the Pyramid of Niches.

"Karen," Peri asked, accepting a mug of coffee, "isn't that one of the buildings you already photographed? The huge one built with all those fascinating openings? I can hardly wait to see it in real life."

Karen gave her a flat stare followed by a shrug. "I don't know how anything in those prints of mine could have fascinated anyone. The negatives I took from here were all too dark."

Giving up, Peri handed her steaming mug over to the gloomy girl, hoping a good strong dose of caffeine would work a miracle.

Josepha, appetite raging, grew tired of waiting and told Esteban to start serving the food, which was eggs scrambled with tomatoes and onions, plus corn muffins and a meat that he called "sausage." It was good, but like no sausage Peri had ever tasted before. As with the meal of the previous evening, Esteban showed a flair for selecting a menu that combined familiar foods with just the right note of regional touches. He was an older man with a hooked nose, and a full, finely modeled mouth. Garbed in his native costume of white cotton trousers and white shirt, he made quite the proper picture of a chef, needing only the addition of a tall white hat—and if one were to be picky about such things, shoes.

By the time the second lot of eggs were ready, Marc and the others had arrived and started filling their plates. Clothes-wise, he had joined the anthropology club, his big, broad-shouldered form attired in khakis and a matching shirt with pockets on both the chest and the sleeves.

"Good morning, Peri Brendan," he said with a nod as he passed her camp chair, the use of her entire name a formality that perversely suggested intimacy. Not waiting for her reply, he sat on the ground beside Karen, directing his next comment to her.

"To what inspiration do we owe the honor of your presence, kiddo? I figured you planned to spend another day hiding out."

There was absolutely nothing in his manner to suggest the deep concern Peri knew he felt for his sister, but the tone he struck was apparently the right one, for Karen at once volleyed back, "I wasn't hiding out!"

"Well, pardon me!" He washed down a mouthful of eggs with black coffee, then grinned up at her, light gray eyes veiled by his dark lashes. "I guess *hiding out* implies there was work you escaped, but except for leaving me to finish putting up your tent, you pulled your fair share of the load."

She glared. "I didn't need you to fix my tent."

"Of course you didn't—not after the slick way you took over mine."

"Funny, funny." Turning her back on him, she got up, carrying her empty mug to the refill pot where she started talking with Theo.

The sibling exchange had been juvenile, but Peri could see how effective it was in breaking down the girl's unnatural reserve.

Seeing her thoughtful frown, Marc made a wild guess as to the reason. "Not like any sausage at home, right?"

Realizing she held a forkful of the sausage suspended halfway between the plate and her mouth, she had to smile. "True enough." She ate the bite thoughtfully, then decided, "Actually, they're much spicier, but what I was mulling over was your conversation with Karen." Feeling expansive, she added nicely, "Since she didn't say it, I will—thank you again for putting up our tent."

The crevice in his cheek deepened and his voice dropped to a wicked purr. "Believe me, the pleasure was all mine. Just think how dull our evening would have been otherwise."

She felt a flush creeping up her throat, but was determined to ignore it. "I'm glad you brought up the subject. It gives me a chance to remind you about my blouse."

His eyes danced. "Not to worry. The job is done."

Startled by his reply, she stared as he polished off the last of his breakfast. She finally found her voice. "You're kidding. You had no time. Not when you were up before dawn, trekking off to watch the sunrise."

"I followed the others later, after I had borrowed thread from Josepha—exactly as you instructed. I'm dismayed you thought I might shirk my responsibility." Looking anything but dismayed, he placed his empty plate on the ground and leaned back, resting an elbow on the seat of Karen's chair. Stretching out his long legs and booted feet in a way that took up as much territory as possible, he radiated total self-satisfaction.

Peri didn't believe him about the blouse and was about to say so when Karen returned, carrying two camera bags. Unceremoniously, she shoved aside her brother's arm and sat down, pulling over a second chair to use as a table.

"Anyone who tries to get into the washroom will find it a madhouse," she reported, sounding almost her usual self. Her braid fell over one shoulder as she opened the bags and started checking through her lenses and other paraphernalia. "Aunt Josepha and the others want to go clomping about the ruins together, and they're all trying to get ready simultaneously. We might as well relax and wait for our turns after they've all gone."

The washroom she referred to had been set up primarily for the use of university students who took field trips during the summer to study the ruins. The facilities were nothing fancy, but thanks to the summer sun on metal storage drums, there was warm water for bathing, a luxury Peri had not dared hope for.

"Sensible plan," agreed Marc with a nod, shifting so he leaned against Peri's chair. "Do I take it that we three will be, as you put it, clomping about together?"

Karen was busy angling a lens to the light, searching for scratches. "Peri and I will be together, naturally. If you want to tag along, it's all right with me."

He rolled his eyes heavenward. "God, it's wonderful to feel wanted." He shifted further, the action putting a shoulder against Peri's jeans-clad leg. "Is all that junk really necessary for just a few pictures?"

Karen declined the invitation to argue. "Go stick a thumb in your eye. Or, if you really need to feel wanted, you can help later by carrying one of these bags."

"Oh, I do need to feel wanted," he answered, surreptitiously moving to increase the pressure on Peri's leg.

With a mixture of emotions, Peri looked down at the top of his head, observing the chestnut glints in the dark brown waves. Her heart constricted. His jests showed how lightly he took their relationship, yet she need only to look in his direction to know that falling hopelessly in love with him had been inevitable.

Forty minutes later, the three of them were following the trail to the ruins, Marc cheerfully toting Karen's heaviest camera bag along with a canteen of water.

They passed a ticket seller's shelter that was no more than a crude collection of splintered planks roofed with dried, curling banana leaves. Beside it was a sign. Peri assumed it would read El Tajin, but instead, it held only the general Spanish term for such a location: *Zona Archeologique*. She was disappointed by this lack of fanfare, yet as they drew closer to the site, her eagerness to see the sacred city increased.

Marc, apparently feeling the same sense of anticipation despite his previous visits, lengthened his stride. Gesturing, he explained, "What makes this place ahead so different from more famous ruins, like the Aztec pyramids in Mexico City, is that the Indians who built El Tajin, have still-living direct descendants."

"Like Esteban, you mean?" Peri asked, a bit out of breath from the uphill climb over rough ground.

"Exactly. The Aztec group is gone, but drawings from hundreds of years back depict Indians with the same facial structure and the same type of clothing as Esteban's. If he could be returned to the time when this all was new, he would fit in perfectly."

The trio rounded a hill of rubble and beheld their first view of the city.

With a gasp of wonder, Peri's eyes fastened on the great Pyramid of Niches. It rose mightily above the strewn earth, stone upon stone, its massive sides forming an arrangement of altars, one for each day of the calendar.

Marc spoke with reverence. "Some of the local natives still worship here and in much the same way as their ancestors."

Karen, who had been busy clicking her camera, paused to call Peri's attention to a pole towering before the massive structure. "That's a steel replacement, so it sort of takes the edge off of all this antiquity stuff, but the Totonac Indians enact an ages-old ceremony in which four young men called *voladores*—the word for 'flyers'—dive off the top of that pole with only ropes tied on their ankles to save them. Tomorrow they will perform for the Sunday tourists, and I should get some good pictures."

Peri wanted to ask more about the ceremony, but Marc was moving on and suddenly she realized that she had been so dazzled by the Pyramid of Niches that she hadn't noticed the many other reconstructed buildings.

For the next few hours they continued exploring, only occasionally catching sight of Josepha, Theo and the others in the sprawled acres of what had once been a great metropolis. After they had explored numerous passageways and shrines and had climbed four pyramids, Peri was more than willing to admit she was bushed. Marc poured out cups of water, and then, while a refreshed Karen went off on her own, he and Peri collapsed on a plot of lush turf shaded by a wall.

Slipping out of her shoes and wriggling her toes in the long grass, Peri looked after the disappearing girl. "You know," she mused thoughtfully, "this morning I wouldn't have taken any bets about Karen, but she surely seems fine now. I honestly think you teased her out of her downhill spin.''

Marc's expression was cynical. "Doctor Josh-along at your service, ma'am. Actually, I don't think anything would have worked had she run too far off her rails. I could have cheered when she started handing back my guff. If she hadn't responded, I had no follow-up.''

His tone told Peri how close to desperation he had felt, yet at the time, he had given no hint. She tilted her head. ''You know, you do an awfully good job of covering up your real feelings.''

One dark eyebrow hooked upward. "Most people do.''

''I suppose that's true.'' They had been sitting side by side, but now she turned herself around so she could see him better, liking the way the sunlight played up the strength of his features. Before he could catch her staring, she refocused, noticing that the wall behind him was carved with strange, idollike figures that had flat, serpentlike heads and ferociously leering grins.

Continuing, she said, ''It's just that you seem to be especially good at camouflage.''

The corners of his mouth quirked in a suppressed smile. ''I'm flattered that you've been trying to analyze me.''

''That wasn't what I was doing,'' she replied defensively, drawing her knees up and wrapping her arms around them, realizing that, of course, he was right.

His chuckle was a deep rumble in his throat. ''Too bad, because if we were going to play Freudian games, I would point out how frequently the topic of our little chats seems to gravitate around buttons and zippers and other such methods of shedding clothing. In fact, if I recall, my first helpful act toward you was assisting you to undress.''

She wrinkled her nose. "You should write scandal for tabloid newspapers. Taking off a coat is hardly undressing." The mention of Freud made her take a second look at the carvings and wonder how all those snaky forms would have been interpreted in Vienna.

Slouched comfortably, Marc toyed with a blade of grass as he smiled lazily in her direction. "Not to change the subject, but did I ever tell you how lovely your eyes are?" Then, answering his question himself, he said, "Yes, I guess I did. But what I didn't tell you was how they affected me that first day. There I was, blithely sailing along until the instant I peered deep into all that wonderful violet-blue. It was like being caught in a whirlpool. All at once I knew you could be one dangerous lady."

She looked at him narrowly, not sure just where the conversation was headed. "I remember that all of a sudden, you just walked off."

He cocked his head, intrigued. "Did I really?"

"Yes, you did." She remembered thinking he had bailed out because he had sensed her dislike. Apparently she had been wrong. She wondered how many other things she was wrong about. Impulsively she added, "My first impression of you was entirely different from the one I have now."

"More analyzing, hmm?" He reached out, idly stroking the grass blade across her instep. "Dare I ask for the verdict?"

"The jury is still out," she quipped, declining to go further.

"Oh, come on." He trailed the grass blade between her toes. "You must have come to some conclusion. At least tell me what you thought at first."

She flexed her foot. "You know how I had you pegged—I made myself clear enough."

"You sure did," he agreed with a grin. "But now, I've apparently redeemed myself. I'd like to know what I did."

"It wasn't anything you did," she blurted. "It was just that I learned about Julie."

He flinched involuntarily, then became as motionless as one of the stone carvings. "What's that supposed to mean?"

The moment seemed suddenly charged with danger, but she could think of nothing to do except to give an honest answer. "It's just that after I knew about Julie and your marriage, I felt—I felt I understood."

Body rigid, his eyes were like gray ice. There was no mistaking his anger. "So all at once, you *understood*. Understood me, you mean. Marvelous. All at once, everything about me lay spread out as neat as a map. I can read it perfectly." Speaking of himself in third person, he mocked, "Marc really is capable of commitment, but he's set up a lot of defenses to deny it, like taking on the role of a playboy. He only acts that way out of a need to protect himself from further hurt." He drew a breath, nostrils flaring. "How am I doing?"

She couldn't blame him for being furious. She had far overstepped her bounds. "I'm sorry," she whispered. "There are times when I just say whatever's on my mind, regardless. I had no right." Feeling miserable, she hugged her knees, wishing she could squeeze herself into a tiny knot and disappear. She managed a bleak smile. "I'm not very much like her, am I?" There was no need to clarify that she meant Julie.

"Not anything at all." His tone was expressionless, but then, with reluctant curiosity, he growled, "Why should that matter?"

She started to say that it didn't, but then threw aside all caution. She was tired of evasions, tired of playing games. It suddenly seemed the time to speak her thoughts and let the chips fall where they may.

"It matters because she was the kind of woman you could really care for, while I—" She faltered, then rushed on. "I had my defenses, too, you know, only they haven't done much to prevent me from—from falling in love with you."

He seemed even more rigid than before. His stare, bleak and unwavering, chilled her. The awful moment seemed to extend into an eternity, and then Peri heard a rattling sound from behind her, a noise like falling pebbles.

"That's Karen coming," Marc announced flatly, getting to his feet.

Mindlessly following his lead, Peri slipped into her shoes and also got up. She turned. There was no sign of Karen. The noise was repeated and Peri saw a heavy-bodied gray lizard scuttle across a rubble pile, small stones shifting in its wake. Startled, she turned back toward Marc. "But that was only a—"

"An iguana," he stated, not meeting her eyes. She realized that all along, he had known no one was coming. He had only wanted an excuse to end the moment. Still avoiding her gaze, he lifted the camera case and canteen. "Esteban should be about ready for lunch. It's time to go."

Numb with pain, Peri followed after him, knowing that her heedless tongue and the mention of the word "love" had been a terrible mistake.

When she awoke the following morning, pain was still her companion. She remembered how Marc had gone to Luis's village immediately after lunch the previous day, and after returning for supper, he had spent the remainder of the evening working on the jeep, which he claimed had developed problems. Peri had no doubt that his only real problem had been devising reasons to keep his distance.

The single bright spot had been Karen's renewed enthusiasm for her project. Paying no attention to what was happening—or more correctly, not happening—between her brother and Peri, she spent long hours talking with the anthropologists and taking exhaustive notes on the sites she had photographed. Theo had been so encouraged by the girl's attitude that he had suggested she might want to consider collaborating with him on a book of horticulture, and now, this morning, after almost literally bouncing out of bed, she had hurried out into the clear, sunny air, eager to begin a new day.

Reluctant herself, Peri took her time getting dressed. She was still inside the tent, listlessly running a brush through her tousled curls, when she heard excited voices from outside.

Hurrying out, she saw those gathered near the breakfast buffet craning their necks upward. Following their gaze, she saw a helicopter swooping in over a low ridge of mountains.

Joining the others, Peri heard Theo say to Marc, "That chopper is coming right on in.... I think it's going to land!"

"It sure looks that way." Marc had to raise his voice to be heard above the roaring thump of the rotors.

Spellbound, the group watched as the machine set down a safe distance from the camp, the long wiry grass of the clearing flattening under the downdraft. The huge blades slowed to a stop. The door opened. The pilot stepped down and turned to assist a female passenger.

"It's Estelle!" whooped Josepha happily. "Who else would appear in such style? I should have known!"

"What's she doing here?" Karen gritted, making no attempt to hide her displeasure.

Peri saw lines harden the girl's softly rounded features as she scowlingly observed the slim form of Estelle Raymond leap lightly to the ground. Wearing a powder blue shirt and matching jodhpur tucked into knee-high tan boots, Estelle looked like a fashion plate.

"She must have come to watch the *voladores* with us," guessed Theo.

"Knowing Grandmother, it's a wonder she didn't decide to steal their show by landing smack in the middle of the performance," condemned Karen. Her sour remark was followed by a gasp as she caught sight of the burly figure who followed Estelle.

"She's brought along Harris!" With stunned dismay the girl watched as her grandmother tucked a hand in the crook of Harris's arm and led him toward the campsite.

Only Peri seemed aware of Karen's unhappy reaction as the others pressed forward to meet the new arrivals.

Gray hair fashioned in a simple but elegant curve that reached to her shoulders, Estelle radiated a condescending charm, her smile the kind a queen might bestow when greeting her loyal subjects. It seemed that everyone in the group already knew her, and in an aside, Theo explained to Peri that she was a heavy contributor to the museum with which the visiting anthropologists were affiliated.

Performing introductions, Estelle, in that cool, somewhat husky voice that conveyed perfect command, announced, "I'd like you all to meet a young friend of mine, the talented architect and builder, Harris Logan."

Thrust into the spotlight, the blond-bearded Harris blushed and squinted, reduced to the nervous mannerisms Peri remembered from long ago.

She heard Marc say in an amused aside to his sister, "Will wonders never cease? Seems our Harris is no longer considered simply a common laborer. Is this Grandmother's way of showing he now meets her exacting standards?"

Karen's answering laugh was harsh with contempt. "It's Grandmother's way of trying to pull the strings." The girl's anger seemed to increase as she spoke. "When I thought I wanted Harris, she was against it because it wasn't her idea. Now that I've thrown him over, she's trying to manipulate things back the other way. All she cares about is controlling people. But it won't work with me!" She stormed off in the direction of her tent.

The helicopter left after the pilot was given instructions to return late that afternoon, and the crowd began drifting back to the breakfast buffet. Harris finally made his way to Peri. "Where's Karen?" he asked, hazel eyes eager. "I thought I saw her with you."

"Well, she was," Peri admitted awkwardly, not really knowing what to say. "I guess she had to go back to our tent for something."

"Peri, my dear," said Estelle, who had followed Harris. She took both of Peri's hands in hers. "How good to see you again." She turned to her grandson, awarding him a smile of praise. "Marc, you must have been taking good care of her. She looks absolutely splendid! And now, where is that granddaughter of mine?"

"Run off to sulk, I would imagine." Marc's words were light, but they held a serious undertone. "She didn't take kindly to your unexpected appearance. And Harris, I'm sorry to say she was especially upset to see you."

Harris's face fell and the look he flashed at Estelle held betrayed confusion, "But you said she would surely be glad to see me by now."

Peri felt sorry for him, knowing how forcibly persuasive Estelle could be. Despite his knowledge of Karen's recent coldness, Estelle must have convinced him he was mistaken. Wanting to believe that Karen would be receptive to his visit, Estelle had simply swept him along with her, believing things would work out simply because she wanted them to. And even now, in the face of Marc's words, she still couldn't accept that she had been wrong.

"Poppycock, Marc darling." Laughing, she patted his arm. "We all know how moody Karen can be. But she's hardly disappointed about my arrival and we know how she feels about Harris. She's just taken by surprise."

Annoyed by her deliberate obtuseness, Marc jerked his arm away. "You didn't catch her by such surprise that she couldn't see through you, Grandmother."

"Oh?" Her catlike eyes widened theatrically. "That certainly makes me sound unscrupulous. Just what little trait of mine did she *see through*?"

Marc's annoyance seemed to collapse into amused defeat. "Your determination to have everyone dance to your tune is one of your most dominant characteristics, Grandmother. It may work fine in business, but it doesn't do so well with your family." He cast a worried glance toward his sister's tent. "And when it comes to Karen, I'm afraid it doesn't work at all."

To Peri's surprise, Karen not only reappeared to have breakfast with the others, but even managed to say a few civil words to both Estelle and Harris.

"Are you all right?" Peri asked her quietly when she got the chance.

"Why wouldn't I be?" Karen demanded archly. Patting her braided coronet of dark hair, she pretended surprise at the question.

Peri studied her narrowly. Although Karen's expression was bland, her eyes seemed to hint at a turmoil of emotions behind a calm veneer. Uneasily, Peri speculated that it might take only a minor incident to set her off again.

Still, the rest of the morning followed pleasantly, with Estelle, who had never visited El Tajin, asking a multitude of questions that the anthropologists practically fell over each other in their eagerness to answer. After lunch and several more hours of conversation on such subjects as tribal human sacrifices, the ritual use of a fermented cactus brew called *pulque*, and the comparatively dull question of whether or not the Totonacs were the original builders of the sacred city, it was time to leave for the performance.

Gathering before the Pyramid of Niches, the group from camp was joined by visitors from several tour buses. Seated to face the plaza, the observers watched the four young flyers and their musical accompanist prepare themselves for what a bus tour guide described as the "oldest ritual in the western hemisphere."

Camera busy, Karen took numerous shots of the brightly costumed performers, who wore gold-fringed, embroidered shawls over white shirts, and red trousers that were also fringed and heavily embroidered. Each outfit was completed by a multicolored embroidered hat festooned with long, colored streamers.

Karen adjusted the lens on one of her cameras as the five men began to slowly climb the one hundred foot pole. Reaching the wooden capstand, the musician took his place while the others affixed the ropes that would hold them secure.

"They won't actually dive off," Karen explained to Peri. "The ropes are coiled so they'll spin down gracefully, twirling around and around as the ropes unwind. It takes a lot of practice and skill to do it right. Some say the ritual started as a tribute to the birds."

Staring upward, seeing the five men clearly etched against the sky, Peri felt shivers ripple along her skin. Without any reference points to remind her of modern life, she realized she was seeing exactly what could have been viewed by a citizen of the ancient Indian world. It gave her a strange, disoriented sensation, as if she had been thrust backward through time.

The music of a flute began, thin and shrill, a monotonous, tuneless sound accompanied by a rhythmic drum beat that stirred a restless, expectant hush in the crowd. Peri felt the music weave around her, it's eerie thread creating a hypnotic pattern that suggested secrets were about to be magically revealed. The poised flyers hung motionless for a moment, then slowly, as the ropes began to unwind, the capstand started turning and the hazardous aerial ballet was underway.

The sight of the ropes was lost against the sky and it seemed to Peri that the men were truly flying free. She watched in awe as the ropes lengthened and the colorful circle of the descending flyers grew wider and wider. Mesmerized by the music and the performance, it seemed to her that the answers to the mysteries of life hovered just beyond the edges of her consciousness. But then, just as these mysteries were about to be revealed, the performance was over. The flyers had reached the ground and their companions were running to assist them.

The applause had already begun before the spell was completely broken for Peri. Dazed, blinking in the sunlight as if just awakening from a dream, she looked around in uncertain confusion. Her gaze skimmed across Estelle, Josepha and the others until she found Marc. Watching her strangely, he moved to her side.

The intensity in his eyes was almost frightening. The bronze of his complexion and the hard, lean lines of his hawk-nosed face seemed to emphasize something primitive, yet irresistible.

"You saw in the performance what I saw, didn't you?" he asked quietly, his deep voice vibrant and sure of her answer even before she gave it. "It was as if something wonderful was about to happen and then, just before it could come into being, it was too late."

She stared at him, stunned by how closely his words matched her own experience. "Yes," she whispered, speaking with difficulty. She moistened her lips. "Yes, that's exactly how it was."

As if somehow apart from the rest of the world, they continued to gaze at each other until Harris's troubled outcry shattered the moment.

"Where's Karen? I know she was right here with the rest of us at the start of the performance. But now I can't find her anywhere!"

Chapter Eleven

As the individuals with the tours dispersed to explore the ruins, it became increasingly apparent that Karen was nowhere around although Harris continued his frantic search.

"I don't see why you two men are being such alarmists, Marc," Estelle complained as the family members stayed behind while the others went to interview the *voladores*. "There can't be any real problem. Karen has probably just returned to camp."

Marc, his face lined with tension, drew a deep breath. His effort to maintain politeness was apparent in the clipped quality of his words. "Things have changed since I spoke with you in Paris, Grandmother. I thought I indicated as much when you arrived, but you preferred not to hear. Karen has been disturbed ever since we came to El Tajin."

"He's right," agreed Josepha. "She's been having those weird ups and downs, and as usual, nobody knows why. Theo will tell you the same thing, right?'' Without waiting for her husband's reply, she continued, ''To have disappeared so fast, Karen must have left before the close of the ceremonies, which is darned odd considering how excited she was about photographing them earlier this morning. I think she's run off.''

The sisters stared at each other, the concern in their expression making their family resemblance startlingly evident despite the vast differences in their manner and degree of sophistication.

Harris returned. Out of breath and half-broiled from exertion under the afternoon sun, he panted, ''I'm going back to camp. That's the only place where she can be.''

Marc nodded. ''I think so, too.'' Eyes narrowed in thought, he ran a hand through his hair. His features looked sharp and his mouth was set in a grim line. ''There's no sense in everyone rushing off. I'll go back with you, and I guess Peri should go as well. Karen seems able to relate to her when she can't with anyone else.''

''You're not going without me,'' decided Estelle. Finally convinced that everything was not as right with Karen as she had wanted to believe, her attitude had completely changed.

''Marc, you may have a point about me being too high-handed,'' she admitted. ''If I misjudged in coming here and bringing Harris along, I owe Karen an apology.'' Her eyes eloquently reflected the pain of self-realization. ''For too long, I may have tried to impose my thinking upon her without listening to her real needs. If so, I'm willing to change, and I want her to know it.''

As the four of them traveled down the rough path leading to camp, Harris was almost beside himself with nervous anxiety. ''Marc, if Josepha is right about Karen running off, where would she try to go? Back to the villa, maybe?"

"Could be." Marc stoically maintained his calm despite his concern. "However, she's hasn't had much of a head start. Maybe—" He broke off as they rounded a hill of rubble and the camp came into view. He halted, chuckling in relief. "She's taken the jeep. That means she won't get far."

Harris looked at him. "How come?"

"I worked on the jeep last night and didn't put everything back. The battery will drain after only a few minutes of driving. Let's go." Elated, he started on a jog toward the campground. "We'll grab the truck and start after her."

Reaching the truck, Marc took the wheel. Estelle slid in beside him, and since the cab seat was narrow, Peri ended up crowded onto Harris's lap, his beard bristling uncomfortably against the tender skin of her upper arm. Marc's assurances that Karen couldn't go any great distance failed to relieve the other man's worry.

"Suppose she runs off the road or something?"

"The steering won't be affected," Marc explained patiently, maneuvering the truck around the curve that led to the main road. "The battery will die out and the jeep will simply stop."

Harris leaned forward to peer out the windshield, anxiously darting his head this way and that, making Peri feel she was shouldered up against a restless porcupine.

"Maybe she'll attempt going ahead on foot," he fretted. "When she sees us, she may panic and try to hide."

"If she does, we'll find her, okay? Four of us to one of her should make it easy. Look—" Marc took a hand off the wheel to point down a long, straight stretch of dirt roadway. "There's the jeep now. Stopped, just as I said."

"Yes! And there's Karen, running just as *I* said!"

The girl was indeed running, leaving the stranded jeep behind as she scrambled up the steep, vine-covered slope that flanked the road. Excited, Harris started to fling open the door of the still-moving vehicle and Peri yelped, clutching for some handhold on the dashboard.

"Wait up, man!" ordered Marc with a roar, and to Peri's relief, Harris obeyed until the truck jolted to a stop.

As Peri and Estelle watched, the men started after the fleeing girl. Marc pulled short at the last moment so that Harris could reach her first. The scene that followed with Harris was reminiscent of how Karen had behaved with Marc that first night at camp, her violent, uncontrolled struggles soon dissolving into wild sobs.

Her coronet had come unpinned during the conflict, the thick braid starting to unplait, drifting glossy, rippled strands across her shoulders. She continued sobbing as Harris, his bearded face a study in helpless misery, led her down to the roadway. He was like a bulky teddy bear who had captured his dark-haired Goldilocks and now didn't know what to do with her.

Leaving Peri's side, Estelle hurried forward to meet them.

Chilly dignity abandoned, she extended her arms, crooning the girl's childhood name, "Kari, Kari, baby. I'm so terribly sorry. I don't know how I did it, but I let you down again, didn't I?" She was crying herself as Karen, after a hesitation, went into her grandmother's arms. The two of them sank down onto the tufted grass alongside the roadway.

"Tell me, baby," Estelle pleaded, holding her close, stroking her hair. "Tell me what I can do to make it better."

"You can't," Karen wept. "That's just the trouble. Nobody can help."

"That can't be true, Kari," Estelle soothed. "Look, we all love you and want so much to help." She looked up at Marc, who had just reached them. "Here's Marc, and I'm here, too. We're your family, baby. Surely we can do something. And if not, here's Harris. You know how much he cares about you."

Karen, burying her face in her hands, broke into renewed sobs. "Harris can help me least of all," she wept. "It wouldn't be fair for me to turn to him when Marc doesn't have anybody. I don't deserve happiness. Not after what I did to him."

"Hey, are you talking about me?" Moving past Harris, Marc knelt beside his sister. His dark brows were drawn together. "What are you talking about, kiddo? You never did anything bad to me."

"Oh, but I did!" Lifting her ravaged face, her voice rose in hysteria. "You were never supposed to know, but...but, what happened to Julie was all my fault! You were so happy together and then I ruined everything. I killed her, Marc! *It's all my fault that Julie died.*"

Estelle gasped and Marc stared at his sister in horrified disbelief. "Karen, that's crazy." His voice was a hoarse whisper. "You had nothing to do with her death, believe me, absolutely nothing."

"But I did!" She reached toward him, then drew back as if she didn't have the right to touch him. Her eyes swam with tears as she cried, "Why do you think I've been so desperate for you to fall in love again? Unless you were happy, I couldn't have happiness for myself—not after the way I destroyed yours. But then, when Peri came, it seemed you two could be perfect for one another. I prayed it would work out so I would be free to

live my own life. Only it didn't. And now, with Grandmother bringing Harris here when I have no right to love
him . . . it hurts so much!" Sobs racked through her once
again. "Oh, Marc, after the pain I caused you, I don't
deserve anything for myself."

Gripping her arms, Marc shook her in helpless frustration. "You're making no sense! Julie hemorrhaged to
death in the hospital. She died because of a miscarriage!
You had absolutely nothing to do with it."

Karen, her eyes wild, cried, "That miscarriage was *my
fault*. The day before, Julie tripped over shoes lying on
my floor. Marc, she fell down! She didn't even know she
was pregnant, but she was, and falling started that miscarriage. *It was all my fault!*"

"Oh, dear God." Marc closed his eyes in anguish, the
blood draining from beneath his tan. When he looked at
his sister again, his expression was tortured. "That's what
you believed all these years? You thought you were to
blame?"

"I am to blame!"

"No." He leaned toward her, his strong face distorted
by emotion. "Karen, you have it all wrong." He spoke
with urgent intensity. "You must understand the truth.
Julie did know she was pregnant, but she told no one. She
became terrified she might die in childbirth, like her
mother. She—she tried to do something to end the pregnancy. I woke in the night and found her unconscious
and bleeding heavily. It wasn't until later, at the hospital, that I learned what she had done. And then, just before she died, she rallied long enough to tell me why."

Karen stared, almost afraid to trust her ear. "But
Marc, I always thought—"

"You only believed what I allowed everyone to believe." His voice was harsh with pain. "Poor Julie would

have never wanted people to know the truth. She was always so proud. Keeping everything a secret seemed best. I never dreamed it would make a difference to anyone." He caught his breath in a long, shaky sigh. "Karen, it must have been awful for you. All these years, punishing yourself for something you had nothing to do with. Karen, forgive me."

Karen stared at her brother as, slowly, the full implication of his words began to impress themselves upon her. Expression transformed, she flung herself into his embrace. "Oh, Marc! There's nothing to forgive." Tears of joy streamed down her face. "I'm just so thankful to learn that I'm not responsible after all."

She wept a bit more into his collar, then blowing her nose on his handkerchief, she started to laugh. "For so long, folks have scolded me for keeping things in such a mess, but I always figured, why bother now, after the damage has already been done? I guess it was a way to punish myself so I would never forget." She gazed at her brother, her round, pretty face tear-streaked, but glowing. "I was so mixed up, so miserable, but no more." She spread her arms with rapturous abandon. "I feel wonderful. It's as if I'm one of the *voladores*, flying—flying so free!"

Marc, his own eyes wet, smiled back at her. "Karen, honey, I'm glad. So very glad." Clearing his throat, he tried to joke. "Hey, does this mean you're going to transform overnight and become Miss Neat and Tidy?"

Karen giggled. "Old habits are hard to break, but . . ." Brushing back her hair, she looked up at Harris, whose face had shown a mixture of emotions as the revelations between sister and brother were unfolded. Her voice became soft. "There is one change I'm going to make—if I'm allowed, that is."

She reached toward the bearded man. After a tremulous moment, as if uncertain he could trust what was happening, Harris grasped her hand.

"Karen?" he whispered huskily.

Standing, her eyes were now only for him. Her voice held a new maturity. "Harris, you've heard it all, but can you understand? I love you. I've never stopped, not for a moment. But can you still want me after the cruel way I've treated you?"

"Of course, honey—how can you ask?" Grinning broadly, he swept her into a bear hug, both of them blissfully unmindful of anything else around them. Then, still wrapped in each other, they moved toward the truck, the soft, joyful sound of their voices drifting back faintly.

"Well . . ." pronounced Estelle, briskness covering her emotions as she stared after Karen and Harris. "That was quite something. There was no way that any of us could have known."

She shifted her gaze to Marc, who was hauling himself to his feet. "And of course, that applies to you as well." Her tone gentled as she looked at her grandson. "It must have cost you quite a lot to hold your silence all those years out of respect to Julie. And today, I suspect it also cost you a lot to reveal the truth."

Peri saw that Marc's complexion was still unnaturally pale. She realized that everything about the pain of Julie's death must have been brought back to him afresh, as if it had just happened.

His muscular shoulders moved in a gesture of defeat. "It was Karen who paid the price, not me. The way I crippled her life is something I'll always regret."

"Nonsense." Estelle was brisk again. "If Karen hadn't been holding herself back, she might have married one of those other two fellows she was engaged to. None of them meant a fraction as much to her as Harris does. Things have a way of working out.''

The woman smoothed her gray coiffure and began brushing dust from her jodhpur with impeccably manicured hands, then paused as a new thought struck. "Good Lord!" Her mouth went round with surprise. "She might have married that banker's son! I handpicked that man, but did you know he's since been charged with real estate fraud?" Her posture became stiffly erect. "Marc, you're absolutely right! I do meddle too much."

Amused despite himself, Marc smiled. "I'm not going to expect you to reform completely, Grandmother. As Karen said, old habits are hard to break."

He glanced over at the truck. "Now, why don't you two see if you can capture Harris's attention long enough for him to drive you back to camp. It will take a few minutes to put the jeep to rights, and then I'll follow."

His eyes touched briefly upon Peri then winced away, as if the very sight of her was unbearable when thoughts of his lost wife were so vivid in his mind. Turning on his heels, he headed for the jeep.

Stunned by all that had happened, Peri stared after him until becoming aware of Estelle's reflective voice.

"To think that none of us ever guessed." She frowned, apparently piqued that her usual shrewd insight had failed. "All these years, Karen's behavior has been such a Chinese puzzle. But once given the vital clue, why all the parts fall together in such an obvious way! It seems impossible that we never suspected. Or that we never suspected about Julie, either."

Mind concerned with nothing except Marc, Peri murmured in anguish, "He must have been terribly hurt. To know Julie was too afraid to confide in him until it was too late . . . so horribly late.''

"Yes," Estelle agreed sadly. That particular aspect seemed to be just coming home to her. "Marc and Julie would have had a beautiful child. One that he would have wanted very much. He had a lot to bear—not only the loss of Julie and the child, but also the hidden tragic circumstances. He suffered far more than anyone knew.''

And is still suffering, thought Peri, walking with leaden steps as she and Estelle returned to the truck. No wonder Marc had shielded himself so sternly against ever falling in love again. Loving Julie as he had, her death must have consumed him with guilt. He probably felt that his love should have saved her from her irrational fears, but it hadn't, betraying them both. Surely it had left a wound that would never heal.

On their return to the campground, Harris and Karen seemed so oblivious to everything except each other that it was a wonder Harris could drive. Disembarking, Estelle laughed, saying to Peri, "That isn't a truck cab we just rode in, it's a cage for lovebirds.'' The enraptured pair had remained behind, still sitting in the truck, lost in one another, as unaware of their passenger's departure as they had been unaware of their presence in the first place.

Seeing them, Josepha and Theo, who had just returned from the ruins with their friends, started in their direction. Estelle met them halfway, assuring them that Karen was just fine.

"I'll reveal the details later," she promised with a wink at her sister. As the married couple rejoined the other anthropologists, Estelle drew Peri aside, her manner becoming serious.

"Since this has become the day for confessions," she intoned, "I think it's time to explain I had more than one reason for sending you to Veracruz." Estelle shook her head, giving a wry, sidelong smile, as if unsure of just what to make of her own behavior. "Peri, that day in the store, I already knew enough about you to be certain you were the one to help my granddaughter, but as I looked down through the mezzanine window of my office, an additional plan came to mind."

Frowning, Peri guessed that Marc had been right after all—Estelle had indeed schemed to use her to detract Harris from Karen. Unsure how she felt about this trickery, she listened as the woman continued.

"I saw my grandson helping you with your coat. Something about your behavior indicated you were strangers to each other and for some reason, I felt compelled to watch. You two talked, then I saw him stop and stare, the oddest expression on his face. It was as if lightning had struck him. Then, he was going off in one direction, and you were going in another, but I knew in that instant that you had captured his attention in a way no other woman had done since Julie."

Hearing Peri's gasp, the woman hesitated, as if steeling herself, then went on. "Despite a fine outward show, after Julie's death, my grandson seemed aimless, as if life held no meaning. My solution was born in that instant I just spoke of, and after talking to you in my office, I was certain. I decided that you and Marc were perfectly suited."

She sighed, her tone deepening with apology. "Marc is right—I tread where I should not. I sent you to my villa, then maneuvered him into being there as well. By dropping veiled hints to Karen in a phone call, I hoped to encourage what I saw as a potentially successful relationship. But, from what my granddaughter said today,

I inspired false hopes in her that made her life even more difficult when my plan failed.''

Estelle's gaze sharpened strangely as she asked, ''Not understanding what was at stake, I played a terribly thoughtless game, didn't I, Peri?''

The question, directed as it was, caught an already stunned Peri off guard. Still digesting Estelle's scheme, she stammered in confusion, ''Well, at least, Karen appears to—''

''I wasn't referring to Karen,'' Estelle corrected softly. ''I saw how you watched Marc this afternoon. You've grown to care for him, haven't you? But perhaps he's not quite ready to return that caring.''

Shattered, Peri knew her face had already told the truth and to deny it would be pointless. Her tone was despairing. ''Even if he was ready, I wouldn't be the one he would choose.''

Dubious, Estelle arched an eyebrow. ''What makes you think so?''

''I just know,'' Peri answered, not wanting to explain it was because she was so unlike Julie, not even wanting to mention her name. Bleakly, she realized that Estelle was still refusing to admit the extent of her errors—not only had she misjudged Marc's ability to fall in love again, she had also picked the wrong girl.

Suddenly feeling desperate to be alone, Peri blurted, ''Excuse me, but I think—'' On the verge of tears, she didn't bother to finish her sentence, but turned abruptly from Estelle and fled to the security of her tent.

Inside, emotions in turmoil, she was about to sink to her cot when she saw her yellow blouse lying there. It was the one she had left with Marc, and she had forgotten all about it.

She stared dumbly, wondering when it had been re-turned. Thinking back, the only possible time had been early that afternoon. Unnoticed, Marc must have dropped off the blouse just before they all left for the performance.

She saw then how neatly the blouse was spread, the fabric smoothed flat, every line precise, making it look rather like a garment for a paper doll. All it needed was little fold-over tabs at the shoulders and waist. There seemed something playful about the careful arrange-ment, a silent testimony to the fact that Marc must have placed it there in a far different frame of mind than his angry one of the day before.

Hope fluttered faintly. It almost seemed that he had been offering an apology. Or was she making too much out of nothing? Seeing that the missing buttons had been sewed back on, she smiled faintly. Then her eyes sud-denly widened. In disbelief, she snatched up the blouse and whirled to open the tent flap, examining the repair work in full light.

Purple thread. And not just ordinary purple, but a screaming fuchsia that Josepha had been using with ad-mirable restraint as an accent in her latest needlepoint design. It was positively the most repulsive contrast with the yellow blouse that Marc could have selected from his aunt's supply of colors. And there was no doubt he had done it knowingly, deliberately. In her mind's eye, Peri envisioned him chuckling to himself as he looped the heavy embroidery thread repeatedly through the button eyes, creating huge glaring knots that he intended to de-fend with a stubborn show of innocence, claiming that he was only following her directions and that color had never been discussed.

She began to laugh. What else could she do with such an exasperating man except love him? She could not believe he would have gone through with such a crazy stunt had he not fully overcome his anger of the day before. No matter which way she viewed it, the return of his bizarre handiwork promised something hopeful about their relationship.

Then she remembered what the previous hour had revealed about his marriage, and how he had dismissed her so curtly on the road. Perhaps the uncovering of his old pain had forced him to acknowledge what she had already feared for so long—that no one but Julie could ever satisfy his heart.

Biting her lip, Peri stood in tormented indecision, then abruptly, she rushed from the tent. She saw that Marc had not yet returned. The timing might be all wrong, but she would go to him. For once and for all, she would learn where she stood.

Chapter Twelve

Peri was five minutes along the road when the home-ward-bound tour buses roared by, churning up clouds of dust. When the air cleared she saw the jeep motoring in her direction. She hesitated a moment. Then, slinging the yellow blouse over one arm, she positioned herself at the road's edge and stuck out a thumb.

The jeep slowly rolled to a stop. Marc, hands relaxed on the wheel, looked her over. The slant of the late afternoon sun bathed her hair in a soft, coppery glow, and played up the translucence of her fair complexion. His gaze traveled speculatively over her simple costume of jeans and cotton knit shirt, neither of which obscured the lush femininity of her figure.

He drawled, "I thought I told you I don't pick up hitchhikers." His face was expressionless.

She lifted her chin. "On the contrary, you said you did it whenever you got the chance."

His scarred eyebrow hooked upward. "And this is my chance?"

She looked at him, the smoky violet-blue of her eyes shadowed by thick lashes. Her voice was as steady and as solemn as her gaze. "It may be the only one you'll get."

Frowning thoughtfully, he nodded. "Then perhaps I better take it." He leaned across the seat and opened the door.

Her knees were shaking as she went around the vehicle. She didn't know what to make of his mood. Thumbing for a ride had been a risk and his droll response was almost too much to hope for. When she had left him earlier, he had been brusque and withdrawn. She had expected to find him still extremely upset.

As she took her seat beside him, he observed the yellow blouse. A quirk of his mouth deepened the crevice in his cheek. "I suppose you've come down to beg a ride to the Better Business Bureau so you can register a complaint. Some people are just never satisfied."

She smoothed the blouse on her lap with trembling hands. "I'm satisfied."

She wanted to say more: to explain she meant she would be satisfied even if he couldn't offer her love, to say she understood that she could never take Julie's place. She longed to tell him all this and more, but the longer she pondered his behavior, the more baffling it became. She knew that the discussion of Julie's tragic death had moved him deeply, yet he now seemed totally composed. Such calm seemed unnatural. It was almost as if he pretended that the scene with his sister had never taken place.

While she was thinking this, he pulled the jeep off to the edge of the road and parked. He reached for her hand. "I want to talk to you," he said, a smile crinkling the corners of his eyes. "Now, before we return to the others."

Troubled, she climbed down from the jeep and allowed him to lead her toward the only nearby shade, a low umbrella of branches spreading picturesquely from what was more of an overgrown bush than a proper tree. Preoccupied, she barely noticed that the air held the haylike scent of greens drying in the sun all day, or that a faint perfume wafted from the small white blossoms that flourished on the vine-covered slope. All she could think of was Marc's mood. He acted as if all their difficulties had been miraculously resolved. Yet they hadn't been. Not by a long shot.

Ducking under the leafy boughs, he pulled her down to sit beside him. The verdant grass cushion was surprisingly fine-textured, and the view of the road was partly screened by a veil of dipping branches. It seemed the secluded bower had been created just for them, yet Peri sat stiffly erect, as if awaiting some signal of doom.

Unaware of her tension, Marc leaned toward her, his open shirt collar showing his broad, muscular throat. Eyes a warm gray in the dappled light, he said, "I've been racking my brain, wondering just how I was going to approach you after my boorishness, and then—" he couldn't suppress a delighted grin "—there you were, hailing a ride! I can't recall a more welcome sight. That is, if you've returned for the right reasons."

He spoke lightly, clearly confident that his desires, whatever they might be, would not be thwarted. Touching her tightly clasped hands with lean, tanned fingers, he continued, "Since yesterday at the ruins, I've acted miserably. I can't imagine what you must have been thinking." Then, stroking her arm, he amended with a chuckle, "Well, yes, I guess I can. I suppose you thought I was a real jerk."

His hand became still as his voice deepened, his manner taking on a serious note. "What you said about loving me threw me for a loop. I was thinking that I didn't deserve your love, but the way I behaved probably made it seem like a rebuff." His gaze was compelling. "Believe me, Peri. Nothing could be further from the truth."

Unable to believe him, she saw the way the strong, chiseled lines of his handsome features were softened by the leafy shadows. She felt he was deluding himself, glossing over serious problems as if they didn't exist.

Taking her silence as encouragement, he went on. "I kept mulling over the situation, getting nowhere. But then, this afternoon, when I saw how the secrets of the past had hurt Karen so badly, everything suddenly became clear. I realized that in my own way, I had been punishing myself much as Karen had been doing. While I wasn't totally without blame, as she was, it still served no good purpose to reject happiness."

He leaned closer, his breath upon Peri's cheek. "I decided that if I wanted a future, I would have to start saying yes." His voice became husky and his hand moved again, caressing her arm as he whispered, "I knew it was time to say yes to myself, yes to life, and especially, yes to you. Peri, I love you."

Those were the very words she had yearned to hear, yet in the light of recent events, they sounded all wrong. With sinking dismay, she felt she understood what had happened to him. With Julie's loss so vividly brought to the forefront of his mind, he was desperately seeking an escape from his pain. In his terrible vulnerability, his claim of loving her was only a reaction, not a true measure of his feelings.

Seeing her expression, he at last recognized that something was wrong. Disturbed, he touched her cheek. "Hey, I'm not so conceited that I expected fireworks and brass bands, but I did figure on a little more enthusiasm than this."

"Marc—" Her words seemed to stick in her throat. "I know you think you're being sincere, but—" She was thoroughly disconcerted by his touch, fingers gently twining a curl by her ear. Moving her head, she blurted, "It isn't necessary that you love me, not if you can't. I don't expect more than you can offer." Close to tears, her voice faltered. "I don't . . . I don't have to have love."

He frowned, dropping his hand. "Peri, if you don't expect love, then what?"

She swallowed hard. "I would rather just know you cared, really cared, than have a pretend kind of love. Whatever you feel for me has to be based on something honest, or it won't last." She closed her eyes, her words almost a whisper. "To begin something and then have it end with us only hurting each other is an unbearable thought. It would be better to have nothing at all."

"Peri, look at me. *Peri*." When she obeyed, he asked in obvious bewilderment, "Pretend . . . why should you say my love for you is only a pretense?"

She felt as if her heart was breaking. "I didn't mean you were doing it on purpose. I know what it's like to have something wonderful—like what you felt for Julie—destroyed. It damages something deep inside. It takes a long time and the right person to make things better. And I'm not the right person—not when I'm so different from her."

A strange sort of shock crossed his face. She knew in that instant he was realizing the truth of her words, and when his mouth narrowed to a grim line, she also knew she had lost him.

His tone was harsh. "So, you've got me all mapped out again?"

The unexpected accusation took her by such surprise that she had no reply.

The aristocratic planes of his hawk-nosed face were cold as he stated, "It wasn't all that wonderful."

Incredulous, she could find only one possible interpretation for his words, but it was one that made no sense. "You can't mean your marriage. I know that—"

He interrupted sharply. "Didn't this afternoon prove how little was known about Julie and me?"

"Well, yes, I suppose," she answered, being cautious, but not backing down. "To a certain extent, anyway."

"To a very big extent," he corrected with sarcasm. He glared at her for a moment, then his face changed, his shoulders sagging. "Peri, I'm sorry." Contrite, he shook his head. "If anything, the very fact that you're so different from Julie is probably what first attracted me. Now that I've figured it out, it seems the truth should stand out in a blaze of neon. Only, it doesn't." Thoughts turned inward, his sigh was resigned. "There's no way you or anyone could know what the marriage was like."

Something in his defeated tone roused Peri to righteous indignation. She tilted her head sharply. "What have we been doing then, running in circles? Of course I couldn't know—I'm not a mind reader. Maybe it's about time you set me straight!"

Without thinking, she had used her best no-nonsense voice. Hearing her imperious order, Marc's eyes widened. Then he threw back his head and laughed. "Pop! There goes my self-involved balloon. Oh, Perdita Brendan, I do love you!"

Still laughing, he seized her in a hearty, exuberant hug that lasted only briefly, because the way she fitted so perfectly into the vital curve of his arms soon completely changed his mood.

Dazed, she wondered just how she had come to be resting back on the soft grass, Marc's mouth so tender upon hers. Then her thoughts, which had scattered in such an impossible way, marshaled themselves once again. Marc's laughter had somehow dispelled the worst of her awful doubts, but she still needed to know the truth.

Pushing him far enough away so she could look at him clearly, she said, "Are you trying to evade the subject or something?"

A subtle hand moved with delicious effect. "Actually," he confessed in a low murmur, "I'm trying to warm the subject up."

Reluctantly, she resisted. "Come on," she said, moving farther away, leaning comfortably on one arm. "You know what I mean."

"Nag, nag." Hitching his big body up against the gnarled trunk of their gnomelike shelter, he plucked a miniature flower from the grass. Using his fingernails to pull the tiny petals, he said in an equally tiny voice, "She loves me, she loves me not . . ."

"She loves you," Peri said emphatically, covering his hand with hers. She was smiling, but her eyes were serious. "Please. It's important."

"Yes, I know it is." Voice deepening, he dropped his bantering. No longer stalling, he said, "It's just that it's difficult—" His eyes took on a faraway gaze. "I guess, like they always say, the place to start is at the beginning—"

The story he told was that of a man embarked on a whirlwind courtship and marriage to an exceptionally beautiful bride who flatteringly behaved as if his every word issued from Mount Olympus.

"Unsurprisingly," he admitted, "after growing up in the company of high-powered women like my grandmother and great-aunt, it never occurred to me that Julie wasn't simply putting on an act. Arrogant as I was, I blithely assumed her slavish adoration was only a wile to delight my masculine ego."

He looked at Peri with troubled eyes. "I never saw that she depended upon others because she felt she couldn't depend on herself. All I saw was her physical beauty and I was too damned shallow to look more deeply. Even so, things might have been all right if her father hadn't died."

When he fell into a pause, Peri interjected softly, "Josepha said she had been very much protected—that his death came as an awful shock."

He nodded. "It...it somehow threw her back into being a little girl again. We had planned to postpone a family for awhile, but that decision soon became academic, because in all the meanings of the word, she lost the capacity to enjoy being a wife. She was like a lovely wisp of fog, without center or substance. And she kept getting worse." A muscle worked in his jaw as he thought back to the painful past.

"Soon her only strength was a fierce pride that precluded our seeking help. Because of that pride, she needed to create the illusion of a perfect life. And I went along with it—probably out of a misplaced pride of my own. My love turned to pity, but I kept thinking that if I were the man I should be, I could help her. I gave her every attention she needed, out of guilt, I suppose, but I gave it."

He paused again, mindlessly shredding the remaining fragments of the white flower. Seeing his pain, Peri regretted she was being so insistent, yet she had to know the rest.

She asked, "And then, Karen came to stay?"

He smiled faintly. "Yes, and I began having hope. Karen was too young to see the flaws, and Julie adored a ready audience for our display of phony perfection. Miraculously, it seemed that Karen's worship was giving Julie the self-confidence she so badly needed. She seemed more stable and ... well, we shared a bedroom again. I remember feeling overjoyed, thinking that Julie and I might have a future after all."

When he continued, his voice was heavy. "Unfortunately, Karen's presence had only inspired Julie to improve the fantasy of our perfect marriage. To her mind, that meant producing a child. It was a plan she kept secret from me, and when she succeeded in becoming pregnant, panic took over. She began brooding over her mother's death in childbirth. And, well ... you know the rest."

His voice trailed off sadly, and in the following silence, Peri consoled, "But you know you weren't to blame."

"Not deliberately, no. But had I handled things differently, the outcome might have been different as well. The thought haunted me. Such a colossal waste of lives— Julie's, mine and that of the unborn child. I figured if I was capable of making such blunders, I had better quit before I made more. Only then—" Mood lifting, he poked the tip of Peri's nose "—I met you."

She tried to bite his finger.

"Lord, woman! You've been hell-bent on maiming me from the start."

He went after her, but laughing, she wriggled away, scrambling from under the shelter and out onto the sun-warmed grass. Bounding in pursuit, he soon captured her in his arms, rolling her over and under his strong body as he threatened, "You're just begging to be taught a lesson, aren't you?"

A few moments later, his breathing uneven, he murmured, "This may take years. I suppose I'll have to marry you just to keep you around long enough for regular classes."

Her heart thumped, but she managed to speak tartly enough. "It would serve you right if I said yes."

He chuckled, his gray eyes brimming with love. "And do you—say yes, I mean?"

"I do."

"You'd better. You have too much to learn and I'm the only one I'd trust to do things right."

And he set about showing her what he meant, but then, after a time, she pulled free. "Time out," she dictated. "I want to know something."

His voice was a stern growl. "This had better be worthwhile."

"A few minutes ago you called me Perdita. I didn't realize you knew that was my first name."

He chuckled. "Perdita Periwinkle?"

His words made her think of her father. Startled, she discovered she could remember him without pain. Somehow, hearing of the ways in which lives could be shaped by unseen forces had brought about a new sympathy. She was through making judgments. Leslie Brendan had been a kind and loving father, and for her, that had now become enough.

Marc was continuing, "It was Estelle who told me your full name. There we were in Paris, up to our necks in important business and she spent half the time prattling about you." His lips nuzzled Peri's neck. "If I hadn't been hanging on every word despite myself, it would have been a real bore." His lips were now at her ear, while his hands were about intriguing business elsewhere. "Usually, my grandmother is all starch and no chit-chat. I don't know what struck her."

Giggling, Peri was about to explain that Estelle had a game of her own, then thoughts of the woman made her remember something more crucial.

"They're going to come looking for us!" She struggled to sit up, her eyes searching the open hillside as if expecting a posse to come into view that very moment. "Estelle arranged for the helicopter to pick her up, and she'll want to see you before she leaves."

He consulted his watch. "I heard her instruct the pilot. We have hours. Two at least."

"That's her departure time. The pilot will arrive earlier."

"So?" he murmured distractedly. Having pulled her down against him again, he was becoming interested in something other than the conversation.

She protested, "That helicopter might fly directly above us."

"Hmm." His expression went deliberately stupid. "Does that mean we leave at once for camp?"

"That actually wasn't what I had in mind."

"Oh?" His brow lifted.

"You see," she said brightly, unable to resist snuggling against him as she talked, "Theo has got me fascinated with the local horticulture."

"Uh-huh. And what does that mean to us now?"

"Well, for example—that funny big plant we were under before." She angled her head to look toward it. "It's almost like a lovely thick umbrella. Now I'm wondering, is it a tree or a bush?"

He gave the matter serious consideration, then, her hand in his, he started to get up. "Easy enough to go back and check."

Minutes later, secure in their bower, they heard a bird song. The melodious trill was as lovely as the promise of a rainbow.

"Well, m'lady, my love?" Marc asked softly. "How's this?"

He gave her that star dazzler of a smile that would have made her agree with anything and everything, although it was probably just as well that he didn't know it.

"Absolutely wonderful," she answered. She smiled up into his eyes, while all around them, the sun's rays through the leafy screen of branches showered them with its magical, iridescent light.

The Silhouette Cameo Tote Bag Now available for just $6.99

Handsomely designed in blue and bright pink, its stylish good looks make the Cameo Tote Bag an attractive accessory. The Cameo Tote Bag is big and roomy (13″ square), with reinforced handles and a snap-shut top. You can buy the Cameo Tote Bag for $6.99, plus $1.50 for postage and handling.

Send your name and address with check or money order for $6.99 (plus $1.50 postage and handling), a total of $8.49 to:

**Silhouette Books
120 Brighton Road
P.O. Box 5084
Clifton, NJ 07015-5084
ATTN: Tote Bag**

SIL–T–1

The Silhouette Cameo Tote Bag can be purchased pre-paid only. No charges will be accepted. Please allow 4 to 6 weeks for delivery.

Arizona and N.Y. State Residents Please Add Sales Tax

Offer not available in Canada.

COMING NEXT MONTH

THE PERFECT TOUCH—Rita Rainville
Psychologist Jana Cantrell was hired to help reduce the stress at
Wade Master's company. She soon found that Wade was causing
her own tension level to rise.

A SILENT SONG—Lacey Springer
When Gray Matthews rented the apartment upstairs, Allegra
determined to keep her distance. She couldn't risk getting
involved with a man who might discover her true identity... or
could she?

ONCE UPON A TIME—Lucy Gordon
Bronwen was a young widow struggling to care for her son, until
an Italian prince rode into her life proclaiming her son his heir
and capturing her heart as well.

REASON ENOUGH—Arlene James
Captain Vic Dayton had very specific ideas about decorum. Coral
defied every convention that Vic held dear, yet it was her
charming lack of inhibitions that eventually melted his heart.

CROSSWINDS—Curtiss Ann Matlock
Amanda was lovely, spirited, sensual... but she was a minister!
Cole found himself inexplicably drawn to her, but could a man
like Cole actually fall in love with a preacher lady?

BEWITCHED BY LOVE—Brenda Trent
Sweet, vulnerable Ashlyn Elliott was a witch. Playing the sexy
witch Ravenna on television created a dual life for Ashlyn, and
Davis Chamberlain found himself falling in love with both of her.

AVAILABLE THIS MONTH: